Rescue

Juliette Renard

French Press

First Edition

Published by **French Press**

Acknowledgements

Thank you to my readers for encouraging me to keep at it. Thank you to my beta readers. And of course, a huge thank you to all the great women who have come before me, and left behind a trail of fantastic books, so that I can follow in your footsteps.

Thank you to all my exes for unwittingly allowing me to borrow some of our steamier moments. Special thanks to Gretchen for telling me I would never finish writing a book – it gave me that much more strength to persevere when things got hard.

Thank you to my father, who taught me to fish, camp, hunt, and survive in the wilderness in the North Woods of Wisconsin. I'm mortified if you're reading this right now, but you deserve the praise.

Contents

1

A Surprise Guest

The mercury dropped well below freezing on the plastic thermometer suction cupped to the window, but for some reason the little cabin always seemed darker and colder than it should be. Granted, it would be metaphorical suicide to step foot outside the door. And if you walked out and waited long enough, it would be literal suicide.

Resting her palm a hand's width from the frosted windowpane, Virginia could feel the temperature shift dramatically. The frigid air penetrated every frosted window in the little cabin: looking into the firs and pines of the north woods, down the white-capped hill, or over the lake behind. The setting sun was a reminder that it was about to get even colder, if such a thing was possible.

Outside, her motorboat was frozen solid into the water, next to the dock with legs that stuck out half above, half below the icy lake. It was the only boat and dock still left in the water, but Virginia had no idea how to take those things out like everyone else. The dock was clearly in sections, and the boat could be pulled ashore if there weren't a shoulder-high rock wall sectioning off the land from the water.

She placed her cold palm, under her shirt onto her heart. She'd taken to skipping a bra because they didn't add any extra warmth, and there were no visitors now. The chill reminded her to stay in the moment, but her hand reminded her how long it had been since any woman touched her there. What she really wanted was something to take the edge off, not another damn exercise from one of her therapists.

But a cold hand was the best she had. That was the idea behind her investing in this cabin. No pills. No booze. Nothing to smoke. Not even coffee. Virginia didn't even like coffee but at least it was something you could have at court mandated meetings while a bunch of losers talked seriously about what losers they used to be.

Cigarettes.

Coffee.

Red Bull.

Anything for a buzz, a bump, a tiny high to remind you how good you used to have it when you had the real thing.

Her phone buzzed.

I love myself.

I am a beautiful human being.

I am worthy of being loved.

Affirmations. Say it and it will come true.

"I love myself," Virginia said out loud. "I am a beautiful human being. I am worthy of being loved. And I'm all alone in a shitty little cabin in the woods like some creepy movie. There's nobody else here to tell me I'm a piece of shit. But I am a piece of shit. Because normal people don't have to go live by themselves so they can stop screwing themselves up. Normal people get to have Christmas with kids, and grandparents, and cookies, and flashing lights, and record players with old music."

The sound of her voice reminded her she was alive. This was all real, and not some bad trip. "And normal people probably don't talk to themselves in their creepy cabins."

Her phone buzzed again, like flashing the message a second time would make the affirmation more real, more true.

Virginia didn't know why she still checked her phone. There was no reception out here. Not even in the closest hint of civilization, a tiny little town at least an hour's walk when the ground was clear.

But the ground was not remotely clear. You could get lost in the waist-high world of white, and nobody would care. Not one person would applaud your efforts to stay clean. Nobody would remember you as the up and coming starlet who always showed up on time, and should have been nominated for an Oscar before she crashed into one stupid building.

People only remember your mistakes.

Scratch that.

The drugs always felt good – they were never a mistake.

Drinking felt good too. And what's the difference between one drink and ten? Like if you make one movie somehow that's totally acceptable, but if you make ten you're addicted to being an actress?

No way. Hollywood wants you to keep making them money until you don't make them money anymore. And then they stop talking to you. You disappear from whence you came, and nobody cares.

People only remember when you do things they don't approve of.

You like to kiss girls when most other girls kiss boys?

We know your type.

You like to be alone when it's in your contract that we follow you with cameras?

We know your type.

And the saddest thing is that they do know your type. They were right about the pills. They were right about missing a huge opportunity by not signing on for a summer blockbuster, that chasing down a meatier role with more depth would only bring out more darkness.

They weren't right about boys. She'd kissed plenty of them in front of the cameras. They were scratchy, impatient, domineering, heavy tongued, and not exciting in the least.

And what a double standard for these power gays to go around fucking any boy they can get their hands on, and then telling her she needed to be dating a boy for publicity.

No thank you.

Virginia knew she liked girls since she was six years old. She wanted to kiss her friend to see what it was like. It felt great. She never stopped.

But for some reason being a girl that likes girls was so complicated. For instance, some girls you fall for don't like girls, and some girls who like girls don't like you. And some girls who like girls and who like you, don't like you when you drink too much and cheat on them, or show up at their house with a stomach full of sleeping pills and tell them to hold you so you can die in their arms.

Something scratched at the front door, and Virginia jumped. It wasn't human.

Maybe a raccoon. Virginia hadn't seen any before, but everyone up here had warned her about making sure all your trash is sealed and locked in your bins, so raccoons and bears don't get at it.

Maybe it was a bear! But bears don't scratch at the door. Do they?

Maybe a wolf. Although Virginia seemed to remember reading that wolves were extinct in the area, and the deer population was out of control. That's why most of the trees were stripped of their bark at the base, because the deer ran out of food in winter.

The scratching came again. Light. Faint. Something small.

What's the worst that could happen if she opened the door a crack just to see?

Animals are predictable. They get hungry. They find food. That's it.

It's people you have to watch out for.

Virginia went to the door and rested her hand on the cool handle. The door was bolted.

Who knows, if it was a hungry bear, and it ate her, would anyone even care?

Virginia twisted the bolt, then turned the knob slowly, quietly. The biting cold of the metal stung her skin. The handle was a perfect conduit to the freezing outside world.

She pulled the door toward her, leaning in so she could peek one eye through the crack.

A black nose thrust toward the crack. Something black and furry scrabbled to push the door open.

Virginia pushed hard, knocking back whatever it was. She closed the door and bolted it once more. Whatever was out there could have rabies, and Virginia had heard about how savage a rabid animal can be on NPR.

Virginia's only contact with the outside world was a CB radio in the corner of the living room, reserved for contacting an old man who brought her groceries. She wasn't about to rely on him for picking up her dumb ass for stitches, assuming they even had a hospital around here.

She walked to the living room to look out at the lake again. Technically she also had a satellite phone for any true emergencies. Stupidity didn't seem like an emergency.

She kneeled on the couch, leaning toward the window. She could feel the extreme cold leaking in on her comparatively warm nose. Two black paws clawed at the window, and Virginia summersaulted backwards, narrowly dodging the coffee table with her head as she hit the floor.

What the fuck was that? She picked herself up and sprang to the window.

Outside, a tiny black puppy leapt up on all fours, scrambling to peer in the window. But it was too short, and the snow-cover on the ground too deep for it to make it all the way up to the ledge.

What the heck was a dog doing at her cabin? How was it possibly alive outside in this bitter winter?

Not her problem. It's probably some crazed stray puppy.

Virginia turned away from the window and surveyed the house.

It was small for her standards, but this is how most people probably lived. It had a master bedroom, living room, kitchen, guest bedroom, two bathrooms (although only one had a shower and bathtub, the other only had a shower), and a garage for only one car, although there was no car in it since she wasn't allowed to drive again. Yet.

She put her hands on her hips. Something was off.

What made Virginia so special that she could decide the fate of another living thing? Maybe that puppy was just down on its luck. Maybe other people judged that puppy, and called it a 'bad dog,' when it was just having some fun?

Virginia's blood ran as cold as the outside of the house. Was she one of those judgmental people that she was so sick of?

She ran back to the door and opened it wide.

A gust of arctic air blew through her shirt, down her sweatpants, and into her only warm parts.

This is such a bad idea.

She slipped her feet into boots, and crunched down on the stoop, holding the wall in case it was icy. It was. She closed the door, and sunk her boots into snow deeper than they were, step after step.

"Holy fuck!" the cold pierced her skin, filled her lungs with the cold feeling of death. She made it around the corner of the house, snow collecting in her hair, and on her shoulders. Around the next corner, the dog laid there, face in the snow.

Dead.

Maybe.

She reached down and touched it. Nothing.

She picked it up, along with a scoop of snow in either hand. It was hard to tell if the thing had frozen to death because now her hands had no feeling.

Lifting the dog to her chest, Virginia circled the house once more, and went inside. She shook off one hand, then the other, flicking bits of clumped snow all over the ground.

"You chose the wrong house, buddy." She closed the door with her hip, kicked off her boots, then carried dog toward the fireplace. "It's freezing in here, too."

A gas fire burned evenly in the brick fireplace. Virginia had neither desire nor skill for anything else, though when spring came around; investing in electric heat seemed like a good idea.

If she decided to stay. That would be madness.

Virginia laid the dog on the warm tiles, in front of the glass covering the fire. It was the hottest place in the house, away from all the window drafts.

The dog had soft black fur that seemed manicured. He was a boy, for obvious reasons. But the breed was harder to tell, a mix of something unique. More likely, Virginia knew nothing about dogs. Like how old was it? No idea.

It seemed too little to be fully grown, but maybe it was a dwarf. Or maybe a newborn giant dog, like a... one of those guard dogs. A black Doberman pinscher. If they start out black. Or are they brown?

He wasn't moving yet, but also not stiff. How fast do dead dogs become stiff? Had she been holding a dead dog?

Maybe Virginia needed to raise her vibration. If she manifested that this dog was dead, would it actually be dead? Maybe she could manifest that it was alive by thinking it.

'Dear dog,' she thought. 'I am manifesting that you are alive.'

Shit. That's not how you manifest things. You have to truly believe them. And you have to focus on the good things. The outcomes.

"Dear dog," the said out loud to the dog. "I hope I'm not screwing up this manifesting by saying it out loud. Maybe that's just with wishes, or maybe it's superstition. I want you to be alive so you can run home, and find your master."

It's got to be better than that.

"I want you to live so you can see that it's a good world. There are good people out there. And even when tough shit happens, there are so many good things to balance it all out, that it's totally worth it to be alive. Don't die at the bad part."

Virginia put her hand on the dog. A warm tear slipped down her cheek and buried itself in her sweatpants.

There's no time for tears.

Her dad said it every time she cried, when she was little. So she made sure there was no time for tears, unless the scene required it.

Regardless, there was nothing more Virginia could do for the dog. She went to the bathroom, and washed her hands. Could you get diseases from dead dogs?

Normally she would just call someone to pick it up. But things didn't work like that out here. This didn't seem like a legit enough emergency to radio for old man Ernie, or try to reach someone on the satellite phone. Plus there definitely wasn't a specialist who could come pick up your possibly dead dog, and not ask you any questions.

Everyone up here was so inquisitive, Jonesing for conversation. What's your name? Where are you from? Are you married?

Virginia dried her hands, and walked to the bedroom. It was time to sleep. That was when time passed the quickest.

Let's get this stupid rehab over with, Virginia. Then we can go back to real life, pretending we're other people.

2

A Mess

Virginia opened her eyes, running her fingers along the most comfortable thousand count thread sheets she was able to import here. Mounds of blankets lay atop her, from the thick white duvet, to an afghan she'd seen at a local spinster's knitting shop and bought on impulse, along with spools of thread, and skeins of yarn she'd also bought on impulse so she would have something to do here.

Two months later, the craft supplies were still in a bag, but the lovely blanket provided life-sustaining warmth in her arsenal of covers.

Rarf!

So, the dog lived through the night.

Virginia pushed the blankets off, and sat up, slipping on a soft pair of indoor slippers that covered the whole foot over her wool socks. She pulled the rumpled covers up toward the pillows. This was as close as she came to making the bed – partly she knew she was the only one who was going to get back in it and, partly she was no longer accustomed to doing menial chores like this since she had a maid back at home who took care of things like this.

She walked down the spiral staircase of the lofty master bedroom to the ground floor living room.

The dog was not lying on the warm tiles in front of the fireplace. A trail of muddy paw prints took a roundabout course from the sofa, to the window, to the kitchen.

Rarf!

And that definitely sounded like it was coming from the kitchen.

Virginia tightened the soft sash around her robe, and followed the faint paw prints.

There was no dog in the kitchen. There however, an overturned bowl of quinoa grits with almonds, and a coffee filter with fresh Capomo coffee alternative grounds sprinkled everywhere.

Virginia had adopted the habit of setting up her breakfast, and organic decaf jungle nut blended coffee substitute in the morning, so that she could wake up with as little resistance as possible. That's what this detox stuff was all about, right? Avoiding all the gatekeepers and naysayers of the world who cramp your style long enough so you didn't have to fill your time with something to dull the pain of fighting back.

When it wasn't some studio exec, or reporter with an urgent deadline, there was always some little detail to take up the devil's costume.

People say they would do anything to be famous. Then when you start doing those anythings, everything becomes laborious. Waking up and trying to figure out what you're allowed to eat to stay strong, and skinny is a chore. Checking your daily schedule to see how many people you will need to meet, with your hair done, in full makeup is exhausting.

Just thinking about it made Virginia's stomach churn with acid.

I don't need to detox from drugs. I need to get away from all those toxic people draining my life force.

On a hunch, Virginia opened the pantry door and out bounded the puppy! He bolted past her until he reached the kitchen door, then slid across the linoleum as he doubled back. He leapt up, sending all four paws careening into Virginia, and they both slid back into the counter.

"Whoa, boy!" Virginia reached for his paws, but the dog lifted them up, over her grasp. "You're a strong one!"

He wiggled through her grasp, leaning in, and licking her neck until she laughed. Then he kept licking her chin, and face.

Virginia tilted her head back, trying to get out of the way of the warm, broad tongue. "Gross. Please stop." She held the puppy as far away as she could, but it continued to lick her wrists, and hands.

"You made it through the night," she said. "You must be starving."

The dog held still, minus his wagging tail, long enough for her to look him over. His face was covered in something brown and sticky, and she realized that now both she, and this dog smelled like his meaty doggy breath.

"What did you get into?" she asked.

The dog hopped down, and ran a small circle. He yipped at her.

Virginia stood up and walked to the pantry. She opened the door and flicked the light on.

Anything glass or canned was knocked on its side. Anything paper or plastic was torn open, with tiny tooth marks embedded. It was hard to believe that something this small could cause so much damage, so quickly.

"You sampled everything?" Virginia's amusement shifted to annoyance in a heartbeat. "What the hell is wrong with you, you little demon!"

She bent down and picked up a box of cereal, leaking corn flakes.

"Seriously, how did you get into all of it?"

Her soft slippers stepped on dahl beans, rotini, teabags, crackers, and god knows what else.

She picked up a tin of sardines, gnawed until the sharp metal lid caved in. The fishy liquid oil mix dripped out onto the floor, where the puppy lapped it up.

"Aha."

The puppy licked its lips and leapt into the air, trying to snatch the tin.

"Oh my goodness." Virginia backed out of the closet, holding the sardine tin away from her body. "So healthy, tastes great, smells so bad."

She set the tin in the sink and washed her hands.

"But we may as well not waste it huh?" She got a bowl down from the cabinet, and opened the sardines properly, plopping them into the bowl. "Since you pretty much ruined all the other food in the pantry."

She set down the bowl, and the puppy leapt into it with its front paws.

Virginia sighed.

The puppy devoured the tiny fish, which proportionately were not so tiny compared to his face.

Virginia picked up a broom, and swept the loose food out of the closet, into the living room, and all the way to the edge of the front door. She opened the door and a chill gust of wind blew inside.

She shivered, and swept all the food out onto the front stoop. Then she closed the door behind her.

"And you," she looked around and found the puppy. She picked it up and held it away from her body. "Need a bath."

She took the puppy to the bathroom, where she proceeded to run a hot bath, and scrub its little body with warm, soapy water. Every time her hand came in to massage his fur, he licked her.

"You're going to make yourself sick, if you eat this soap."

Her phone buzzed, and she glanced back at the sink counter.

I am calm.

I feel good.

I am in control of my life.

The puppy hopped up, scrambling out of the tub.

"Wait!" Virginia grabbed for him, but it was too late. He was already out the door, tracking soapy water down the hall.

"I am calm." She grabbed a towel.

"I feel good." She walked into the hall, following the wet footprints.

"I am in control…" she walked into the bedroom. "No! Get out of here."

The puppy was up on the bed, rubbing its face and fur into the nest of blankets on top.

Virginia popped the towel down on the puppy. "I am in control of my life. Not you, me." She lifted the puppy inside the towel. "And you are not allowed on this bed. You're not even allowed in this room."

She brought the puppy down the stairs, and into the living room. She set him on the ledge of the fireplace. "This is a good place to dry off. Not in my blankets."

The puppy wriggled his way out of the towel and shook, splattering little water droplets on Virginia's face.

"Lay down," Virginia patted the ledge.

The puppy sniffed her hand.

"Stay." Virginia walked to the kitchen. She opened the pantry, which looked like nobody had cleaned it up since she left the mess sitting there. Logically, it made sense. But she was so used to Gosia doing everything: tidying, cleaning, tucking in sheets, making beds, preparing snacks.

Where was Gosia now? Seriously, where was she? Virginia didn't leave any clear instructions after the accident. It was all a blur of lawyers, and settling out of court. The whole cabin-in-Wisconsin idea stemmed entirely from her agent Callie.

Now that the winter snow and wind sealed her in here, Virginia knew why. This was a punishment. Admittedly, Virginia was a high-maintenance client, and there were scads of luxury rehab programs that had actually furnished her with drugs.

At least Virginia's mom was getting some sick satisfaction knowing that her daughter was suffering, and not living the dream life that her mom had always longed for, but failed to achieve.

Unlike most faces in the industry, Virginia wasn't related to anyone famous. Her mom had tried for most of her youth to break into the scene, working her way into the pants of anyone in a power position. But her lack of ability, coupled with her manicured beauty that wasn't enough to turn studio heads, ensured she never landed so much as a speaking role.

Virginia had inherited that grim do-or-die determination, but her genes contained some next-level beauty, and raw talent that begged for a performing career. Combined with a little luck, and a lot of help from people along the way, she had made it as far as you can before the star life starts imploding.

She looked down. She was holding the broom again, standing there idle. She pushed all the way into the pantry, picking up bottles and cans. Not all the food was ruined, but considering it was hard to get anything she legitimately liked around here, the packages were a huge loss.

It looked like it was time for a trip into town. She could replace her dwindling provisions, get some actual dog food, and see if she couldn't find who his owner was, or at least were she could dump him, and still have a clean conscience.

Of course, getting to town would be a problem. There was a car in the garage, which wouldn't help anything because even if her license hadn't been revoked, the unplowed snow outside would go up to the windshield anyways.

She could just walk. That's what people used to do before they invented cars.

How could life have been harder back then than it was now?

Virginia closed the pantry door, and locked it. Why was there a lock on the pantry door? Maybe the previous owner had a dog that pulled the exact same thing bullshit.

She looked around the kitchen. What else would that little puppy get into and destroy while she was gone? She began setting things up on counters, theoretically out of reach.

"Hey dog," she called. "I'm going to go buy food for both of us in town."

She walked to the living room. The puppy was not where she had commanded it to stay.

"Dog?"

She collected her winter gear, wrapping herself in warm scarf, and a big jacket. She grabbed a hat, and mittens. Then she laced up her long, leather snow boots.

"I'm leaving, dog. Please don't break anything while I'm gone."

Virginia opened the door a crack. The biting cold was fierce, even when the sun was out. The shade from the evergreen trees blocked most of the light, and the wind whipped what little spirit she had out of her body.

She went out the door, and closed it behind her.

'We need food,' she thought. 'And I can't just live with a dog because it showed up here. He has to go somewhere else.'

Her foot crunched into the snow. It wasn't waist deep after all. It was freezing. It was beautiful. She continued up what used to be a cobblestone sidewalk that led to a dirt road. Both were covered in snow.

At what she assumed was the edge of her property, the snow got deeper. That made sense, because she remembered that her land was raised up above the street level when she arrived in the autumn. 'Street level,' was a funny term. All the roads this far into the backwoods were made of dirt, and gravel. And now just thick layers snow.

In the distance, a loud buzzing sound approached. Over the horizon line of a snow capped hill, a snowmobile appeared. The rider was decked out in winter gear.

The snowmobile buzzed down the hill toward Virginia.

It was probably some obnoxious northern beer-gutted dude.

Virginia stopped in her tracks, watching.

The snowmobile slowed, as it pulled closer. The engine idled as it sidled up next to her.

"Do you need a ride?"

A woman's voice. Husky, but female. She was wearing a jacket so thick it made her look obese; her face was covered by an actual ski mask that muffled her voice, with goggles. She had at least one hat, and a fur lined hood pulled down over it. Her gloves were like racing gloves with stripes, but puffy. The overall lack of matching colors or any central theme resembled a character from *Mad Max*, except in the snow.

Virginia shook her head.

"Where are you headed? Town?"

Virginia nodded.

"You won't make it there before dark. Hop on." The woman reached her hand out.

Virginia accepted her hand, and climbed onto the back of the snowmobile. Hopefully, this was a good decision.

"Hold on tight."

Virginia grabbed the sides of the woman's jacket.

"Tighter."

Virginia wrapped her hands around the woman's waist, delicately placing her hands on the fabric.

The snowmobile revved, and took off much faster than she had anticipated.

Virginia leaned in and clung to the woman in front of her. Her butt thumped up and down, as the vehicle sped through the forest.

Trees and bushes flew at them, as the woman twisted and turned, artfully dodging them. They were definitely not on any road anymore.

Virginia closed her eyes, her heart pounding. The wind whipped at her face, attacking any exposed orifice. She pressed her whole head into the back of the woman's jacket.

3

Spider Junction

There was something about the vibration of the giant machine and the pressure of her crotch landing on the padded seat as they thumped along, that was sending an all too familiar message to Virginia's pleasure center.

She realized that she didn't need to be holding on as tight as she was to the woman in front of her. But it felt good. It felt so natural to be inadvertently rubbing up against the heavily cushioned ass of this complete stranger.

With a little luck, the woman wouldn't even notice that Virginia was enjoying it. And if she never read the tabloids, she would have no idea that Virginia was openly gay, and purportedly, a floozy. Although, that last part was debatable. A girl had to have some fun, right?

It had been way too long since she had hooked up with anyone for that label to stick. Part of kicking the addiction was letting go of the late nights, which included hedonistic girl parties. Once Virginia arrived in Wisconsin, her options had all but vanished completely. She'd given it all up, cold tuna.

In fact, the closest she had come to anything remotely resembling a woman was the ill-dressed grizzly bear that she was holding onto. A woman who despite her somewhat butch appearance, was just a gruff product of the woods. She probably lived alone, drank whiskey, and ice fished for her dinner.

But that didn't stop Virginia from enjoying the heat, as she held on for dear life.

The forest thinned, and the snowmobile pulled into what passed for a town. They rode up to a snow bank, and the woman stalled the engine, which resembled parking.

Virginia could see that they had taken the path through the trees because the roads here were plowed. And snowmobiles probably couldn't ride on plowed streets. Maybe they could. That obscure fact was outside of her knowledge subset.

"You can let go now," the husky voice said.

Virginia flushed, despite the cold. She quickly removed herself from the snowmobile, and stepped deep into a drift of snow. Leaning back, and pushing the top layer with her hands, she freed her boot as her butt sank in behind her.

The woman on the snowmobile removed her goggles, and pulled up her facemask. Underneath, her face was angular, strong. She wasn't thin, but neither was she nearly so thick as the padded winter clothing suggested. Her pale skin looked like it had never seen the sun. Her light blue eyes, and shocks of almost bleached white hair suggested Nordic descent.

"Are you lost? It's not a very big town."

Virginia shook her head.

"Sage." The woman extended her gloved hand.

Virginia offered her mitten and was greeted with a forceful handshake that took her by surprise.

"I'm Sage." She repeated. "Do you have a name?"

Virginia realized that Sage was regarding her with a special look reserved for small children, and idiots. She stood up, and snapped to attention.

"I'm… Virginia," she offered. She wasn't used to giving out her real name, but nobody recognized her up here. "I think the cold got to my head. I'm not used to it."

"Can I buy you a drink?" Sage asked. "It'll warm you up."

Virginia stared back blankly. "No thank you."

Sage's features dropped slightly, but visibly. Most people would have missed it, but Virginia picked up on any social nuance.

"I don't drink," Virginia added hastily. "Not anymore. I'm trying to quit."

"Quitter," Sage smiled. The wrinkles at the corners of her eyes and the fine lines above her mouth hinted that she was in her mid-forties, and possibly a smoker. She turned, and walked away.

"Thank you so much for the offer," Virginia called after her.

Sage was right, it would have been a hell of a walk to town.

Virginia ambled down the snowdrift, moving slowly to avoid slipping. Apparently her gorgeous boots were missing an essential element that everyone else's seemed to have: rubber grips on the bottom. At least if she fell, she would be the best-dressed person falling.

A number of shops lined the main street of Spider Junction, which was named after the equally creepy nearby Spider Lake. Luckily, Virginia was far enough away to live on Lost Hollow Lake, which although it shared a waterway, did not induce the nightmares of spiders crawling out of the water, and into your bed at night.

There wasn't much to see, or do here. The few dozen stores down Main Street were still decorated in Christmas themed boughs, ribbons, lights, and bells. Most of the shops were closed because not surprisingly, the dead of winter in January was not tourist season.

She walked the length of the street, just to stretch her legs, and warm up. Despite the plowed road, there were no cars driving, nor parked.

The grocery store wasn't hard to find. It was also the hardware store, pharmacy, and post office rolled into one. She walked into the dim lighting, and picked out a basket. It was so small; they didn't even have shopping carts. Inside, it was warmer than outside, but not by much.

Virginia looked around. Everything was crammed into narrow shelving, to make up for the lack of space. A number of animal heads hung from walls, and a giant taxidermy bird that might have been an eagle was hanging in the center, with it's talons outstretched like it was about to kill something.

Replacing her food stores would not be entirely possible here. The narrow aisles shelved mostly candy, potato chips, soda, and popcorn. It went without saying there was no 'gluten-free' section, although they did have canned dog food next to the tuna, and sardines.

The old man Ernie that did her weekly shopping must go all the way into the next biggest town of Hayworth, where the grocery store actually had a produce section.

Virginia slowly perused the shelves. Every item on her list seemed to take forever to locate, as there was neither rhyme nor reason to the haphazard placement of anything in there. Slowly, she managed to find things that either she, or the dog, would be able to eat.

Virginia picked up a can of Red Bull, which amazingly they actually had. Her mind spiraled down a number of pathways at the same time. Chugging vodka Red Bulls until she decided to turn the club into a strip show, and make-out contest. Watching the sunrise from a crowded hot tub on a yacht deck, everyone sipping Red Bull sadly because the last of the cocaine got knocked overboard, and it was all they could do to hold Virginia back from jumping into the Pacific ocean to rescue it.

Virginia put her hand behind her neck, massaging it. The weight of her winter clothes felt like it was cramping her shoulders. She breathed into it. Pain was only a feeling.

There was plenty of booze for such a tiny shop. Crown Royale, Bombay Sapphire, Absolut Citron, Fireball, Jägermeister. They even had Grey Goose. At least people knew how to drink, up here.

It felt like hours of poking around the little store, while Virginia's only company was her memories. Eventually, she hefted her basket onto the counter, where the lone cashier read an Archie comic quietly to himself.

Virginia set the cans down loudly, to get his attention. "I found a puppy, or more accurately this puppy found me. What should I do with it?"

The cashier was an expressionless, chubby teen with a haircut from home, and glasses so thick he appeared comical. He looked inside the basket, and picked up a can. "Pedigree is a good brand. It depends on what kind of meat your dog likes, yeah? Does he like chicken? Or beef?" His northern accent was thick, but still intelligible.

Virginia shook her head. "I don't know. I mean I don't want to keep it. Is there like a pound, or something around here?"

The cashier set the can down, and looked at Virginia. "Why don't you want your dog?"

"He's not my dog," Virginia smiled politely.

Don't be irritated. You're better than that.

"He's a stray." She pantomimed with her hands. "I just need to put up a lost dog sign, or something. Maybe the owner can take him back, or anyone that wants him."

"Why don't you want him?" The cashier was young, innocent, not even flirting, which was unusual when people saw Virginia. His line of questioning belied possible mental incompetence, and his lack of interest in her beauty backed that up.

"You're right," she agreed, to nothing in particular. "But if anyone tells you they're missing a cute little black puppy, would you let them know that I found it?"

The cashier smiled simply. "Sure."

Virginia realized that not only did he not know her name, or how to contact her, but that even if he did, she had neither phone reception, nor Internet to be able to respond. Not an entirely well thought out plan on her part, but at least she had two big bulky bags of groceries to carry through the woods now.

The cashier tied the plastic handles tightly, and knotted them so the contents would not spill out.

Virginia handed him an old school credit card, since of course, they did not accept Apple Pay. She watched as he set the card into a chunky plastic machine, and pressed down on a swipe that created a carbon copy of her card on a piece of paper below.

She didn't know such a thing ever existed. She signed the paper, and the cashier handed her the card, along with a huge receipt on yellow copy paper.

Virginia walked out of the store, and ran straight into someone. Her feet slid on the icy sidewalk, and she scrambled to catch herself as the weight of her bags pulled her down.

"Excuse me," she managed. She looked up and saw a black ski mask looking down at her. Instinctually she gasped, and retreated.

"Are you scared of the mask?" That husky female voice again. Sage pulled the ski mask up over her face, revealing her pale white skin. "It's pretty common for people to wear these when it's this cold out."

Virginia breathed, her heart started again. "I'm so sorry, it didn't realize it was you. Where I come from, people only wear those if they're going to pull out a gun.

Sage patted the side of her jacket. "I'm not pulling out my gun unless I need to."

Virginia glanced down, then back up at Sage's face. She was serious. She actually had a gun concealed somewhere.

"I'm going home. Thought you might want a ride back."

Virginia stood there looking into Sage's face. Should she accept a ride from a gun toting maniac snowmobile driver who just got done drinking at the bar? Her other option was to walk into the forest carrying two heavy grocery bags, with no road, no map, no GPS, no phone, and the sun setting shortly.

She nodded, and smiled. "Thank you. Is it okay if I bring these?" She lifted her grocery bags.

Sage reached down and grabbed the bags out of Virginia's hands. She walked over to her snowmobile, and opened a surprisingly spacious storage compartment at the back.

Virginia hiked up the snow bank, trying to keep up with Sage.

Sage set the bags down on top of a half empty bottle of whiskey, and an actual handgun. Then she closed the compartment, until the lock clicked. She turned the key in the ignition, but nothing happened.

She produced a rope from somewhere under the seat, then proceeded to wind it around some metal gear up at the front of the vehicle. She pulled the rope taught, then yanked at the cord, and the gear started spinning.

A low rumble turned into the purring of a happy motor. Exhaust flooded the air around them, dark and thick against the cold forest air.

Sage put the rope back under the seat and swung her strong leg up and over.

Virginia was both delighted at the prospect of holding on and riding this bumpy machine, while still terrified of dying. She hopped on behind Sage, and rested her gloved hands around the woman's midsection.

This was going to be interesting.

4

Denzel

The snowmobile whipped around more violently than the last time, cutting through thick layers of snow, and sending it spraying off in its wake.

Virginia couldn't get into the rhythm of the jarring speed and sharp turns. Was Sage trying to make it uncomfortable? Surely the alcohol, and fading light from the setting sun weren't helping her navigate what appeared to be an infinite number of trees and snowy hills that were all identical.

Sage slowed, riding abreast of a shallow snow bank that led up to an unshoveled walkway. The last of the sunlight gleamed off of Virginia's cabin windows, the golden light making it appear more like an enchanted cottage than a cold, miserable means to keep her out of trouble.

The entire ride couldn't have lasted more than thirty minutes, but it made Virginia seriously question her ability to gauge distance, as well as her now laughable idea of walking through the cold wilderness to town.

She let her arms relax, and slid off the vehicle.

Sage got off the other side, leaving the motor running. She came around and unlocked the storage compartment.

Virginia picked her bags up out of the compartment. "Thank you so much. I don't know what I would have done without you today."

Sage locked eyes with her through the eyelets of the still creepy ski mask. She reached for the bottle of whiskey, and twisted the lid off. Jim Beam. Cheap, but tasty.

She pulled up her ski mask, and took a long drink from the bottle. "Such a sad story." She nodded toward the cabin.

Virginia looked from the cabin back to Sage. "I never met the people who lived here. My manager bought me this, sight unseen."

Sage nodded, sadness washing over her face.

Virginia was taken aback by this vulnerability, Sage didn't seem like the type. "Did you know them well?"

Sage took another long drink. "Doesn't help anyone to tell sad stories when they're over." She screwed the cap back on, and placed it into the compartment. "And you don't look like the kind of girl who has problems, so I don't know if you'd get it."

Virginia resisted the urge to retaliate. Sage had been kind to give her a ride to and from town. But how selfish was she to think she was the only girl on the block with problems? Had she ever had to deal with losing her loved ones? Been accused of partying in a culture that basically tells you that you have to party to fit in? Told she would never really make it, no matter how hard she worked, and how much she achieved?

Sage tossed a nod her way, then climbed back onto the snowmobile, carving her way up the hill. She disappeared over the ridge, but the whirring was still audible after she left.

Fuck that. Good riddance.

Virginia tried to follow the footprints she left earlier in the day back to the house, to keep any more snow from sneaking in over the top of her already wet and cold boots. When she reached the door, she saw the food she had so unceremoniously swept outside.

Not good. Something's going to find this.

She fumbled to get the warm key from her pocket into the frozen lock. She took off her mittens, to get a better grip.

The key would not turn. "Oh come on!" she hissed. She tried: twisting the opposite direction, turning the handle as she twisted, jiggling the key.

Then it struck her. It might just be cold. She placed her palm over the lock, warming it with her body heat. The searing cold from the lock back to her palm was excruciating.

Virginia breathed into it.

I love myself.

I am a beautiful human being.

I am worthy of being loved.

She relaxed her shoulders, breathing deeply.

In.

Out.

Her mind wandered to a party at Venice Beach, maybe a year ago. A bodybuilder was slurring his words, talking about being the toughest guy anyone had ever met. Virginia laughed at that, and challenged him to a contest of who could put their arms into the ice chest for longer.

They both stuck their arms into a beer cooler, filled with drinks, ice, and frigid melted water. Admittedly, the guy lasted about eight minutes before his face turned sour, and he yanked his arms out. The poor sport said something about it being harder for him because he had bigger arms.

Virginia just smiled and kept her arms in the ice chest another two minutes, just to rub it in.

She smiled now, too. This lock had nothing on her.

She put the key back inside, and twisted.

Click.

The cabin was much warmer than she remembered, even in the entryway. She closed the door, and slipped off her boots, setting them on a mat designed to hold snowy outerwear.

The house was quiet.

Virginia slipped off her wool socks, replacing them with her plush house slippers.

She walked to the kitchen, and set the grocery bags down. No dog.

She checked by the fireplace. No dog.

She checked the hall. No dog.

She checked the stairs. No dog.

With the sun down, the house was darkening quickly. Virginia turned on the lights as she went from room to room.

In her bedroom, the puppy was curled up in her nest of blankets. His ears perked up when he saw Virginia, his tail rapidly wagging so hard it audibly thwapped against the bed. His little pink tongue happily lolled out of his mouth.

"Aha." Virginia leaned down, picking him up in her arms. "I thought I made it clear that you were not allowed to be in this bed. Even when I'm not home, which is like, never."

The puppy licked her arms, pawing up her chest so it could lick her face, as well.

"Alright," she winked her eye, pulling the puppy away from her face. "Hold on."

Virginia carried the puppy down the stairs.

"I did it." She walked into the kitchen. "I went to town all by myself." She thought about that for a moment, reflecting. "But I also had some help, from a grumpy old bear named Sage."

Virginia leaned into the puppy's ear, and whispered, "she's not a people person."

The puppy yipped. She set him down on the counter.

"You're right," she conceded. "I shouldn't talk shit about anyone behind their back. And it is kind of hypocritical to be locked in a cabin in the woods, and accuse her of not being a people person. The difference is, I don't like being alone out here."

She set the puppy on the counter. "Okay. Before I show you what I picked up in town, you need a name."

She set both hands around the puppy's body.

The puppy licked her hands, and wrists.

"I'm going to call you a boy name," Virginia pondered. "Like John. Or... what's a good boy name? Will? Like Will Smith? No, that's racist. I love Will Smith, but I don't know. Are you not supposed to give a black dog a black name? Denzel is a fucking cool name. I've never met Denzel, but he's a solid choice for a lead."

The puppy barked.

"Okay, feedback. Bark once if you like Denzel for your new name." Virginia demonstrated by nodding her head. "Bark twice if you don't like it." She shook her head.

She inched her face closer to the puppy. "Denzel."

He looked at her with his baby blue eyes. He cocked his head to the side as she got closer.

"Once for yes, twice for no."

He licked her nose.

"Nose licking was not an option. I will assume you like the name Denzel as much as I do."

He barked.

"See? One bark! That settles it."

Virginia lifted Denzel down to the ground.

"Alright," she opened the grocery bags, unpacking the cans and boxes. "These are for you." She set stacks of cans on one side of the counter. "And these are for me." She set a few boxes of pasta and one can of Red Bull on the other side.

Virginia picked up Denzel's bowl from earlier. The sardine meat around the edges that he hadn't licked clean, were now hardened into a crust. The smell reminded her of walking through Bangkok on her one trip to Asia, before she decided she would never go back.

In retrospect, at least Bangkok was warm.

She picked out a new bowl, and opened up a can of dog food. She emptied the contents into the bowl, and the can made a sucking noise as the column of meat slid out, and air sucked back into the can.

"Yummy." She set the bowl down in front of Denzel. She read the can. "Beef and liver dinner in meaty juices."

He sniffed it, and looked up at her. He yipped.

"What?" Virginia pointed at the bowl of food. "You're not hungry? That's good stuff. The guy at the store told me so."

She bent down and lifted the bowl toward Denzel's face.

Denzel jerked his head and neck away from the bowl.

"Come on," Virginia coaxed. "Eat it, it's totally good!" Some of the wet food pressed against the fur around Denzel's mouth. "Plus I could have died out there trying to get to town today, which ultimately was for you. I have plenty of people food here for me."

Denzel licked his chops, but backed away. He yipped again.

"Also, I was trying to find your owner." Virginia pressed her lips together. "Which may be impossible, since there's no way to communicate with anyone up here. So you're stuck with me for a while."

Denzel yipped, hopping up on two legs.

Virginia thought for a moment. She took out a second bowl, and opened a different can of dog food. "Chopped chicken and rice?"

She plopped the contents into the bowl, and set it on the ground.

Before the bowl even touched down, Denzel pushed in, eagerly devouring the mix.

Virginia watched, impressed as he wolfed down mouthfuls of the foul smelling meat. "Well, I guess everyone in the world does have something to teach you," she mused. "You must not like beef."

5

Yet Another Surprise Guest

Virginia's eyes popped open.

Something was scratching at her door. She sat up in the darkness. The moon had a hard time penetrating the huge trees surrounding her cabin, and she had unplugged any light-polluting source so that she could sleep in pitch black. Right now that was more frightening than comforting.

More scratching. It was coming from outside her bedroom door.

She closed her eyes. Hopefully, if she just ignored him long enough, he would go away.

The scratching persisted.

Nope. I'm not playing this game.

Denzel yipped.

Virginia opened her eyes. Apparently she was playing this game.

She yawned, and checked her phone.

1:27

Way too early to be getting out of bed.

"Go away, Denzel," she called softly.

Denzel yipped again, scratching at the door to add emphasis.

Virginia kicked at her covers. Was this just some test from the universe to see how much she could handle? Here she was trying to be good. Trying to get to sleep early every night. Doing her damnedest to just keep a low profile and a clean system. And now there's another being that would literally be dead without her, that she didn't ask for, and couldn't get rid of.

"Alright," she stepped out of bed, and into her slippers. "I'm awake. You better have a good reason to be outside my door."

She opened the door.

Denzel ran past her in the darkness.

She could hear the faint thump of him hopping up onto her bed.

"No," Virginia hissed. She groped around the blankets for him. As soon as she touched him, Denzel started licking her hands. "I don't care how cute you are. You can't sleep in this bed. It's mine."

She picked him up, cradling him in her arms. "I'm sick, don't you know that? There's something wrong with my brain, and I'm a bad person. I'm trying to get better. And I need to sleep."

Denzel's tail whapped against her forearm repeatedly.

Virginia carried him down the stairs, walking slowly to keep her balance in the dark. It would be all too easy to miss a stair, and turn this into a real fiasco.

One time, she'd seen a girl in heels roll an ankle as she was walking down a staircase to an underground speakeasy. The poor thing grabbed for air, and came down head first, hitting about every other step on her descent.

Virginia remembered laughing at the time, her mouth, and cheeks so numb she couldn't feel them. She thought the girl might actually be dead, but somehow deep inside, that didn't seem like such a bad thing. A ticket out of here, a free pass. It's not suicide if you didn't mean to do it. How lucky was that girl in a crumpled heap, lying at the bottom of the staircase with blood leaking out of her nose?

Every part of that experience should have tipped her off that she was out of control. What kind of psychopath laughs when they see that happen? Virginia had looked around, and seen that her friends were laughing along with her. There were the hottest girls in the club, all sitting at a bottle service table cracking up while the people below them went into panic mode trying to help out.

Virginia focused her eyes, standing in what felt like the doorway to the kitchen. It was even darker downstairs. She didn't remember walking here, but she must have. She entered the kitchen, holding up Denzel so their faces were almost touching.

"It's time for you to sleep, Denzel. You can't sleep in my bed. So I'm going to lock you in here."

Virginia set Denzel down, and closed the kitchen door carefully. She let out a long, slow breath.

Denzel scratched at the closed door. He yipped.

"No, my friend. It's time to sleep." Virginia walked back toward the staircase.

But then she heard an odd sound. It was almost like something else was responding to Denzel.

She spun toward the front door.

Denzel yipped, still scratching.

But now the other thing made a noise too, like a… chirping. But not a cricket.

It was coming from outside.

Now would be a perfect time to have a peephole on the front door, like any other normal house. Unfortunately, the door was solid wood. The cabin didn't even have a front porch light, which Virginia mentally noted she needed to add these things come spring.

It didn't sound big. Or dangerous.

Virginia slowly twisted the freezing cold metal handle. The door latch slid noiselessly all the way open. She pulled the door open a crack.

It was too dark outside to see any movement.

The cold air seeped in through the crack.

The night was quiet. Peaceful.

Behind her, Denzel barked. It was more than a yip this time.

Virginia started to close the door, when the chirping came again.

She flicked on the inside lights, and squinted as the house lit up. She opened the door wide.

No less than three pairs of glowing red eyes looked back at her. They skittered about, all of them chirping in harmony.

Denzel barked like crazy now, scratching at the kitchen door with all his might.

Virginia stamped her plush slipper on the floor, noiselessly. "Get out of here, you... things!" She leaned out the door, and made a whooshing motion with her arms.

One of the things dared to come closer, chattering its teeth, challenging Virginia's authority over this forest. As it climbed the stoop, light spilled onto it. An enormous raccoon, its greedy claws holding a box of corn flakes. For a split second, it seemed like a creepy commercial for children's cereal.

No, this was real life.

Virginia instinctually pulled herself back into the house. She slammed the door closed, and bolted it. She leaned her back against the door, as if to block the raccoon mob if they decided to break it down. But nothing like that happened.

"All of you need to get on out of here!" she called out. "You're not welcome to steal that... garbage." Although in a way, they were kind of doing her a favor by cleaning it up. And the food was going to go to waste anyway. There wasn't even a compost up here.

Why did she care so much about controlling the raccoons?

"Scratch that," she added. "You can take the food, then go home."

Where did raccoons live? It didn't matter, they needed to take their loot, and go back to wherever they came from.

Virginia turned the light out. It seemed even darker than before. She closed her eyes, to let them adjust.

Denzel yipped again, to let her know that yes, he was still locked in the kitchen.

"Let's everyone take a deep breath," Virginia inhaled deeply, letting the air out slowly.

I love myself.

I am a beautiful human being.

I am worthy of being loved.

Maybe she was becoming more conscious. The old Virginia would have fought those raccoons for no good reason, because she believed they shouldn't be stealing her food. They were cleaning up garbage, like nature's little ferocious trash men that also get in your face when you tell them off.

The old Virginia might have shut her door on Denzel and never thought twice about him dying out in the cold.

Virginia puzzled it out. Maybe you repeat the affirmation to remind yourself to do those things – to be those things. Like, 'I am becoming a person who loves myself, so don't forget to practice self-care.'

Yeah! She was on to something.

'I am becoming a beautiful human being.' It was never about her looks. It wasn't a reminder that she had a great body. It was about the things she did, the way she treated other people, and even animals.

And she was becoming worthy of being loved. Why would anyone have loved her when she walked around being an entitled asshole all day and night: smashing things, trying to get a fix, shit-talking her peers, using her celebrity status to hook up with chicks who could care less about her?

Virginia laughed out loud. She'd expected some flash of light, or a blue dot or something to come with a revelation like this. Yet here she was sitting alone in the darkness.

She opened her eyes, and walked to the kitchen door, opening it.

Denzel came flying out, smashing into Virginia's legs as he tried to rub up against her.

"Alright," she bent down and scooped him up. "It's bed time. And yes, you can come sleep in my bed. Quietly."

She ascended the stairs, and set Denzel on her bed. She pushed off her slippers, lying down in the quiet room.

Denzel was thrilled with the new arrangement. He licked her neck, her chin, her mouth, and nose.

"Nope," she put her hand up to guard herself.

He licked her fingers.

"No licking."

He pushed his wet nose into the webbing of her fingers, and licked her palms.

"Oh my goodness." Virginia pulled Denzel close and snuggled him, holding him so tight he couldn't escape her embrace.

Denzel wriggled.

"I can still hear you licking the air." She let go of Denzel, sticking both palms under her pillow. She turned her face toward the edge of the bed.

Denzel sniffed around for a moment, then contented himself with walking in circles until he'd discovered the coziest spot to sleep.

He was finally quiet, and still.

But sleep was not so easy for Virginia.

Maybe it was all the commotion. Maybe it was all this sudden change in what had been an incredibly boring life in the cabin. She didn't even have time to make tea yesterday. She hadn't even glanced at her phone except to check the time when Denzel woke her up.

Virginia hadn't had a phone free day in who knows how many years.

Was it too late in life for someone to love her?

Like, after all this fluffy affirmation self-love, changing who she was – was it too late? Had she already burned all the bridges? Was there anyone out there in the real world that gave a shit?

Then it all turned inward. All that insecurity was really just a reflection of herself. Who did she care about? Her self-obsessed mother who always belittled her? Her two sisters who refused to talk to her anymore? A small following of addicts, booty calls, and friends with benefits? They would all be gone once they found out she was clean.

Her agent Callie didn't count, because she got paid when Virginia got paid. This whole cabin lock down sobriety camp had actually been her idea. Her relatively exact words were: "*Virginia, honey. I'm with you for the long haul. But at this rate, you aren't going to make it for any haul.*"

It stuck in her mind because Callie's mild Southern twang made "any haul" sound like Virginia wasn't going to make it for *Annie Hall*. All she could think about in that moment was that maybe they were going to do an Annie Hall remake, and she was wondering who they were going to cast for the Woody Allen role, if she were to play Annie.

46

Callie spent a few months running this plan by Virginia, over and over, until it became their idea. And then after the accident, it was the only idea.

6

Losers Weepers

The sun was bright when Virginia opened her eyes. She wasn't used to waking up late, since starting her habit of tucking down early. Not doing copious amounts of coke, or staying up to see the sunrise was also helpful when trying to wake up early.

She blinked away the sleep. Did she really almost fight a raccoon last night? Her divine revelation about her affirmations came flooding back to her. Was it brilliant, or was she just tired?

Virginia reached over to the side table. She flipped her phone face down, then tucked it into the drawer beneath the table. Today was going to be a phone-free day. Maybe tomorrow too. She would have to see how long she could keep the streak alive.

She pulled the blankets back, ready for a gust of cold air, but the house was pleasant. She slipped her feet into her plush slippers, and walked to the door. At the edge of the staircase, she looked down.

Denzel was perched on the couch, his two feet on the sill of the window. His triangular muzzle pointed motionlessly out toward the frozen lake.

Do dogs usually do this? Was he watching another animal, or something?

Virginia descended the stairs slowly. Noiselessly.

As she reached the ground level, she looked outside the window to see what he saw. It was a clear day, and appeared warm for the north woods during this season. There was no movement outside, no animals, no people, no clouds. It was like a painting: the colors vibrant and alive despite the lack of life.

Virginia walked up and placed a hand on Denzel, who startled at her touch.

"I wonder where you came from?" she mused, scratching behind his ears.

Denzel reveled in the affection, but his gaze was still focused on something out there beyond the walls of the cabin.

"You weren't such bad company after all," Virginia adjusted her sash, walking toward the kitchen. "I guess you are allowed to sleep in my bed after all. But only so you don't wake me up with your incessant whining."

In the kitchen, she clicked on the electric kettle. She reached up and took an almond milk tetra pak from an entire cabinet filled with them.

"Are you hungry?" she called to Denzel. She poured almond milk over her granola. "Of course you're hungry, you're a dog," she said to herself.

She opened the cabinet where she'd set his food. Twenty-two cans left, twelve chicken, seven meatloaf, and five beef. He was going to have to make do when the chicken ran out, because Virginia was not making another trip into town just to satisfy his picky eating habits.

She finished her granola, mixing the boiling water with the coffee substitute. The aroma of roasted dandelion root, nutty and rich, filled the air. Fresh cinnamon blended in, a nod to holidays, and always perfect for this wintery weather. While the steam curled off the thick brown liquid inside the mug convincingly enough, it was not coffee by any stretch of the imagination.

Virginia had taken to adding a dash of maple syrup, and almond milk to her morning blend. She drank real coffee black, but since this was not real coffee, it required a bit of doctoring up.

It was like the truth. Nobody wants to hear the actual truth about themselves. You can lay down the bare facts, and no matter how scientifically accurate they are, the human body will not accept them... unless you stir up your truth with a little maple syrup, and almond milk.

Virginia smiled at her musings, stirring her 'coffee,' while absentmindedly groping a can of chicken and rice dinner, which at this time of morning was more truthfully a chicken and rice brunch.

She set the can opener to the lid, holding her breath to ward off that tinned meat smell when she popped the seal. Winding the handle around, the can spun, which surprisingly, started a mechanical whirring sound.

Virginia circled the lid completely, then let go of the can opener.

The mechanical whirring continued, growing louder.

She smiled. It was only a coincidence that the can opener and the noise started at the same time. But what was it? Was the icemaker frozen? That would also be oddly strange, considering how cold it was here.

Then it clicked. It was that snowmobile from yesterday, somewhere outside. Possibly approaching, since it continued to increase in volume.

Virginia looked at the kitchen doorway.

Denzel was happily chewing on something.

"Where did you get a bone?" Virginia sipped her coffee drink. Then she set it down, too hard. "Hey!"

It was not a bone.

She lunged for Denzel, but he scampered away toward the living room.

Virginia ran after him, dodging the door, the corner of the wall, the lounge chair.

But this was Denzel's game. It almost looked like he was smiling, the way the corners of his mouth curled up on either side of the whitish object in his mouth. He was not chewing on a bone. It was an object that had been wrapped neatly in toilet paper, and stuffed in the bathroom trashcan, where it was intended to stay.

In fact, the only reason that said object was still sitting in the bathroom trashcan and had not been removed from the house entirely, was precisely so that animals would not dig it out of the trash, nor chew on it.

A knock on the door: hard, and formal.

"Drop it, now!" Virginia lunged again, but Denzel dodged under the legs of the rickety chair that came with the place, and probably should have been firewood, except that it was a gas fireplace.

He went for the doorway, with Virginia right behind him.

"Denzel," she put her hand out. "Give it back."

Denzel dropped the tampon.

Virginia reached for it.

Denzel snatched it up before she could reach it.

A knock on the door again, but louder this time.

Denzel ran back into the living room with his prize.

Virginia unbolted the door, opening it a crack. She peered out.

Sage stood outside, her ski mask pulled up to reveal her ruddy cheeks. She pushed the door open, shoving Virginia backward. "People don't usually lock their doors up here."

Virginia stood blocking the entryway, her hand on the door handle. "I do."

Sage looked her up and down. "If the lock freezes, it can be hard to get in. Or out."

"Noted." Virginia stood there. She relaxed her shoulders, breathing out as she did so. "I very much appreciate your hospitality yesterday."

Sage nodded curtly. "I think you have my dog."

Virginia breathed deeply. "I may. What does your dog look like?"

Sage pointed past Virginia. "That cute little half Boxer, half Lab mix with a tampon in his mouth."

Virginia flushed, her deep breathing asphyxiated by her throat clamping down. She looked down, and sure enough, Denzel was sneaking up behind her, his chew toy firmly locked in his meaty maw.

"Bartleby!" Sage knelt down.

Denzel dropped the tampon, and jumped into Sage's arms, licking her face.

Both women stood there awkwardly for a moment, realizing where that tongue had been only moments earlier.

"How did you know he was here?" Virginia leaned against the door.

Sage rubbed Denzel all over, her long hand caressing his tummy. "Curtis told me."

Virginia looked at her blankly.

"Curtis, the cashier. You talked to him yesterday. You said you wanted to send Bartleby to the pound." At that, Sage's demeanor shifted.

Virginia shrugged it off, shivering in the chill wind the door was letting in. She must have vastly underestimated Curtis. "Actually, I've really been enjoying Denzel's company. I know he likes cans of chicken and rice dinner, and not beef and liver dinner in meaty juices."

Sage scowled. "Bartleby doesn't eat canned food. He eats venison, with little cooked vegetables chopped in."

Denzel licked Sage's chin. Traitor.

Virginia nodded slowly. This woman was trying to steal her new friend. It was hard to imagine that he had only come to her two days prior, because now she was trying to imagine how lifeless the cabin would be without him. "Denzel and I have formed a very special bond over the last few days."

Denzel's ears perked up. He righted himself in Sage's arms, coiling up like he was about to pounce at Virginia.

Virginia lifted her hands to catch.

"You mean Bartleby," Sage put one hand in front of Denzel's chest so he couldn't jump.

"Denzel," said Virginia. "Like Denzel Washington?"

Sage shook her head.

Virginia threw back her head. "You know, the actor. Training Day? The Hurricane? The Manchurian Candidate?"

Sage looked at her blankly.

"Let's see... Malcolm X?"

"I might have seen that," Sage conceded. "I don't really pay attention to who's in a film."

Virginia mused. "So you have no idea who I am?"

"You're the woman who found my dog." Sage's features softened. "I can't thank you enough for taking care of him. He's very special to me." She paused, stroking Denzel. "People tell me I come off as gruff, at first. But I want you to know how much I sincerely appreciate this."

Virginia tried to conceal her smile, but her face brightened against her will. Vindicated. "Of course." She shrugged. "It's what anyone would do."

"No," Sage said. "You probably would have died walking to town to get him food. Not everybody would be so reckless." She took a step back, holding Denzel.

"Wait," Virginia leaned out the door, closing the distance between them. "Could we have a play date sometime?"

Sage stared at her.

"Denzel and I. Obviously." A shiver ran up Virginia's spine. It was more than the air outside, which was not as cold as usual.

"What do you mean?" Sage asked. She looked confused.

"I just want to hang out with him once in a while." Virginia sighed. She could breathe deeply again.

"I guess so." Sage retreated another step. "I could come back in a few days. If you want that."

"Yes, please." Virginia flashed her million-dollar smile. "I have coffee substitute, and maple syrup, and almond milk."

Sage raised up one open hand powerfully into the air.

Virginia waved goodbye. An engulfing aura of sadness washed over her. It felt palpable. She watched as Sage mounted her snowmobile.

Denzel peeked up over her shoulder and yipped at Virginia one last time, before the engine started, and they cut through the snow, ascending the hill.

Virginia watched them zag through the trees. It was no big deal, right? She just met Denzel, and only yesterday she was still trying to give him away. She wanted to find the owner, and now the owner found her. And obviously Sage was a great owner.

So it's no big deal.

Virginia closed the door. The granola soured in her stomach.

I love myself.

I am a beautiful human being.

I am worthy of being loved.

None of it sounded true.

She picked up her stupid used tampon, wet with doggy drool, and threw it.

What she really needed was some excitement.

Virginia checked the medicine cabinet, in the downstairs bathroom. The mirror opened, and the shelves inside were completely bare. Not even an Advil.

Thank you, smart Virginia from the past. You knew that future shitty Virginia would poke around trying to justify needing one thing or another, and fuck this whole thing up.

That is definitely not what we need right now.

Was eleven AM too early to tuck down for bed?

She cracked her only can of Red Bull, and savored the sweet fizzy bubbles.

7

Play Date

Virginia looked out the back window, over the lake. The ice looked less solid. There were more birds out now, pecking around the snow like they might have missed something.

The animals somehow knew that winter was breaking. It was like they possessed some intelligence beyond human comprehension. Or maybe they just had nothing better to do with their time than stay in touch with the weather patterns.

It had been a few days. Three, to be exact.

Was Virginia being needy? That was one of her pet peeves with her girl friends back at home. When they had nothing going on in their lives, they would invent these little dramas to keep them mentally occupied. Things like whether some girl had called them, or not called them, or what pet name they called them. Or needing to hang out with someone else's puppy that you just met two days ago.

She was being needy! Fuck. What a needy little bitch. No wonder Sage was weirded out by the play date request. The smart thing to do in her shoes would be to never come back, just ghost Virginia.

But she did seem genuinely grateful.

Come on, Virginia. Don't overthink things. Life is simple, there's no need to get in your own way.

Go make breakfast.

Go for a walk.

Do yoga.

Breathe deeply.

But the window beckoned, the gas fire burning quietly in the hearth behind her.

This was what Denzel was doing the other day. He wasn't watching anything in particular, just looking into the deep beauty of the world around him. How much time do we spend looking at our phones? Looking at our walls? Closing ourselves in, away from this great big wonderful wide world that we were born into?

A familiar whirring sound in the distance broke through the meditative morning quiet.

A snowmobile!

Virginia hopped up, and ran to the door. She ran her hands down her jammies, smoothing out the wrinkles. Then she reconsidered.

She ran to the staircase, bounded up the steps two at a time, and flung open the dresser in her room. Normally, she would balk at taking off her warm layers, but today she stripped down, and slipped on a presentable dress. Not having to sit in front of the mirror for an hour to have her makeup done was a welcome change. She kicked the warm jammies under the bed.

The engine noise outside drew closer, then stopped.

Virginia bounded back down the stairs, running for the unbolted front door. She opened it fully, and watched Sage walking toward the house. There was no puppy in Sage's arms.

"Good morning," Virginia said. Her eyes searched Sage.

"Hi," Sage walked up on to the stoop. She was enormous, at least six inches taller, and twice as wide. She slipped her backpack strap slowly off her shoulder, and Denzel's adorable face peeked out of the top.

Virginia gasped; her face couldn't contain her delighted smile. "Denzel!"

Sage let the name slide. She unzipped the bag, and Denzel hopped out onto the snowy step. He bolted inside the house when his paws touched the cold.

"Would you like some coffee substitute?" Virginia asked, her eyes following the little black streak tearing around her house.

Sage reached into her backpack. She pulled out a small brown bag, and a carton of milk. "You offered that last time. I brought real coffee, and milk, in case you're out." She handed the ingredients to Virginia.

"Please, come in," Virginia took a step back to make way for Sage. She walked slowly toward the kitchen. "Make yourself at home, and let me know if you need anything."

Sage stomped the snow off her boots, brushing the loose clumps off the bottom of her pant legs. She stepped in, and closed the door behind her.

Virginia followed Denzel into the kitchen, and turned on the electric kettle.

Denzel yipped, and flung himself into the folds of Virginia's dress.

"Don't let him fool you," Sage called, removing her boots, and snow attire in the entryway. "He had a huge breakfast."

"You're not going to fool me," Virginia smiled. She opened the door of the refrigerator and took out a bowl of leftover tuna salad. She set it on the ground, and Denzel eagerly chowed down on the meaty mayonnaise.

Sage walked to the doorway of the kitchen, scrutinizing the house. "I like what you did with the place."

Virginia stood there holding two mugs. "Oh, wow."

Without her boots, and snow gear, Sage stood a few inches shorter. Her unruly naturally bleach blonde mane hung down over her broad shoulders. Her voluptuous breasts rebelled against her soft sweater, while her curvy hips pushed at every end of her vintage corduroys.

She was no grizzly bear. She was a Valkyrie sent down from the Nordic gods on a snowmobile.

"What?" Sage checked her clothes, to see if she spilled something.

"I thought that you…" Virginia's thought trailed off. "I like your outfit."

Sage hesitated, waiting for the sarcastic follow up. "Thanks, I like yours. Not very practical, but it's a good reminder that winter won't last forever."

Virginia poured the real coffee into her French press, then added the now boiling water.

Sage looked down, and noticed Denzel with his face pushed into a bowl.

He looked up and licked his chops, missing a great deal of the meat emulsion coating his chin.

"What do you do when it's warm out?" Virginia set up a plate of crackers, and cheese, with little Italian mini-biscotti, and Belgian chocolates.

Sage shrugged. "Same thing as when it's cold. I write."

"Oh, you're a writer?"

Sage looked up, her hand lightly brushing her chin. "Velvet Gloves, Finger on the Pulse, Heat in the Darkness?"

Virginia stared blankly. "Those are books?"

Sage relaxed, and smiled. "You've never heard of me?"

Virginia smiled back. "Touché. I guess I don't read books as much as I read scripts." She poured their coffees. "You like milk in yours?"

"No. I brought the milk because I didn't know what almond milk was, and I don't know that I care to find out."

Virginia handed her a hot mug of coffee. "Are you being serious with me right now? Do you guys not have lactose intolerance up here?"

"Thank you," Sage set her coffee on the counter, and produced a metal flask from her pocket. She unscrewed the lid, and poured in what smelled like whiskey. "I don't have a lot of company up here. I love this place. It's perfect for finding some quiet time to work, but truthfully, I'm not from around here."

Virginia took the tray of treats in one hand, and her coffee in the other. "Oh, where are you from?"

Sage followed her from the kitchen to the living room. "I'm from up north, where it gets really cold."

Virginia set down the tray, and the mug. She smoothed out her dress, and sat on the couch. "You're not joking, are you?"

Sage shook her head. "Manitoba. My daddy used to take me fishing down here every summer; it was his favorite place on earth. And he was my favorite human on earth."

They sat in silence for a moment. Virginia couldn't think of anything to follow that up with.

Denzel ran in from the kitchen, excited about the prospect of a lap seat. His face was smeared with tuna salad wherever his little tongue couldn't reach. It made the little fur around his beard look prematurely grey.

Virginia laughed, and grabbed a napkin. "Oh my goodness. Come here." She patted the couch with her free hand.

Denzel hopped up obediently. He closed his eyes, and tilted his head back patiently as Virginia massaged his snout with her napkin.

She crumpled up the grimy napkin, and Denzel hopped into her lap.

"You mentioned that Denzel is really special to you." Virginia sipped her wonderfully hot real coffee. "How did you find him?"

Sage sipped her coffee, as well. She reached down and helped herself to the chocolate. "I was there when he was born."

"Oh, that's so neat!" Virginia felt herself drawn to this woman. No matter how guarded she was, it was like everything she said was a mystery story with more than what you bargained for hiding just a breath away. "Where was that?"

Sage savored the chocolate in her mouth, considering the question. "My house. Not far from here." She set her coffee down, and leaned in. "In a way, Bartleby's mama was a gift from my love. We used to hike through the woods every day, the three of us."

Virginia nodded slightly, her mug pressed to her lips. "What happened?"

Sage clouded over, breathing out. "I don't think you want to know."

Virginia leaned in, mindful of the cozy little puppy sleeping on her. "I do! You can tell me about him."

Sage scanned Virginia's face. "I don't think so. It's not a happy story."

Virginia shifted her weight. "Tell me. I'm not as delicate as you think."

Sage narrowed her eyes, taking a big swig of coffee. She alternated with another swig from her metal flask. "There was a girl who used to live here, at this house. She grew up in this small town. Had a mom, and a dad. Pretty normal life. Religious."

Virginia nodded.

Sage continued, slowly, deliberately. "I would hang out with her every summer when we were kids. She was my best friend when I was in town. She was my best friend, period. I hung out with other kids up in Manitoba, but not like this. Sometimes she spent the night at my place, sometimes I spent the night here."

Sage looked at the ground. Deep breath. The muscles in her cheeks clenched. "I don't know when it was that I realized it was more than just friendship. We were older then. I think we both knew all along. We had this deep bond, some magical connection not of this world. We shared the same dreams sometimes."

The expression left Virginia's face. She sat there blank, mesmerized.

"To say we were in love was one thing, but it was more than that. Our lives, and our beings were connected. In a way it was the sweetest, most innocent thing you can imagine."

Sage rocked back and forth, gently. "My dad was so happy for me. He figured it out before anyone else. Didn't even ask me about it, he just knew."

Virginia cleared her throat. "I've never experienced anything like that. It must have been so…"

Sage's eyes misted. "It doesn't end well."

Virginia swallowed. "I'm sorry. I'm listening. Go on."

64

"Her family was super religious. She went to church with them when she was little, but she never really bought into it. It was like there was her church going side, and then there was us. She never muddied the waters, so to speak. And whatever we had was spiritual in its own right."

"But..." Sage licked her lips. "Her dad didn't see it that way. I guess he was suspicious, because he read her diary. He, uh..."

Her lips trembled. "It happened so fast. He kicked down the door of my house. His gun was pointed at us before I had time to scream. I didn't know what was going on before I heard the first shot."

She shook her head. "Nobody knew. My dad ran in from the kitchen, and just reacted. He did what any loving father would do. I wasn't even watching... I couldn't take my eyes off the gun pointed at me."

Virginia's misty eyes were wide. "Holy fucking shit."

Sage shrugged, wiping tears from her cheeks with the back of her hand. "There was everyone I loved and held close in this world, lying on the floor. And I was standing above them, alive. It wasn't fair.

She took a deep breath, trying to collect herself. "I never saw her family again. I heard her dad was arrested, but I never testified. I just... couldn't. It was like my spirit left with them that day, and never came back."

Virginia sniffled, wiping tears from her cheeks too. She nodded appreciatively. "Thank you."

"Sorry," Sage offered. "You asked."

A chill ran down the back of Virginia's scalp, all the way through her shoulders until it felt like the chair was reaching for her. Something was tugging at her heart, like an icy tendril from outside had snuck in and punctured her body.

"So," Sage rubbed her hands on her corduroy pants. "We should probably get going. Before it gets dark." She stood up, looking around. "Can I help you tidy up?"

It was hours before the sun would drop, but Virginia didn't want to overstay her welcome, even though it was her house. She was the one who had requested a play date. She put both hands under a very comfortable Denzel, upside down in her lap, his face mooshed into her stomach.

He lifted his head lazily, cute red tongue dipping out of his mouth.

"I can manage," Virginia kissed Denzel's forehead, then stood up, cradling him in her arms. "It wasn't too weird today, was it?"

Sage walked to the entryway, shaking her head. "We could do this again. I'll spare you the drama next time"

"Okay," Virginia smiled, following her. "I would like to see you soon. Do you mind returning in a few days?"

Sage smiled back. "Sure." She put on her thick padded pants, her boots, and her jacket. The grizzly bear version of her was back.

"Okay," Virginia helped a very cooperative Denzel into Sage's backpack. "Thank you so much for coming over, I appreciate the company."

"Me too." Sage tenderly shouldered the backpack, and stepped outside, crunching into the snow. "You know, if you leave food lying out here the raccoons will come."

Virginia looked at the fresh batch of corn flakes poured on the ground. "I left that there for the raccoons. They're my friends now."

8

Lost

Virginia's eyes popped open.

Something was wrong. Someone else was in the house.

She lay under the covers, the black of night thick, and dark.

Silence. But she could feel the presence of someone else. Something else.

Something strange, something unnatural.

Not scratching.

Not a dog.

Not the raccoons.

Her heart raced. Was she just dreaming?

Footsteps on the staircase. Was it Sage? Why would she be here at night? And without her snowmobile?

Silence. Crickets. Something outside. Maybe just the wind.

Should she call out, and ask who was there?

The footsteps came back. They grew closer, louder. They reached the top of the landing.

Virginia's door was already open a crack. She sat up, trying to peer under or around the door for feet, but it was too dark.

She needed a weapon, or something. Anything other than just laying in bed, waiting for whatever was out there.

She slid noiselessly from under the covers, picking up a wooden hairbrush.

Not enough. She fumbled for the bedside lamp, ripping the cord from the wall.

"Who's there?" she called out.

Silence.

Virginia lifted the lamp, ready to strike.

She pulled the door open slowly.

There was nothing in the hall.

But something tapped the window behind her.

Her heart froze. She turned around, but it was too dark to make anything out.

Maybe it was just a little moonlight sneaking through the clouds.

Virginia looked down the stairs, into the darkness. There was no moonlight tonight.

She flicked on the lights in the bedroom. "Is somebody in here?" she called again.

She ran down the stairs, jamming her hand into the light switch at the base of the stairs?

"Hello?" she called.

She ran to the kitchen. And then she heard it. Someone was above her, on the second floor. Someone was coming for her, and fast.

Virginia ran for the front door. She flung it open and ran outside, screaming.

She looked wildly about, her bare feet crunching through the icy snow. She sped through the darkness, feeling the steep incline of the hill. She had to get away.

Virginia chanced a glance back at the house, fading into the distance.

No lights outside. She couldn't even see where the house was anymore.

There was no way to tell if someone was chasing her.

She pushed on until suddenly she smashed her face into something, hard.

Virginia lifted the lamp, bringing it crashing down in front of her. "Get away from me!" she screamed into the night air.

She lifted her other hand to defend herself and touched the rough bark of a tree.

She held on fast to the broken lamp, her hands shaking. Her feet stung. Something warm and wet was leaking down her face.

Virginia looked around, trying to let her eyes adjust. But it was too dark.

Adrenaline pumped through her veins, but the icy sting of snow melting under her feet, and the wind whipping through her pajamas cleared her head.

"Hello?" she called. Her voice was steadying itself.

She needed to get back to the house, but where was it?

Where was she? And if she did make it back, would that person, or that thing still be inside?

Virginia dropped the broken lamp, and set both arms out in front of her. She had to do something; she couldn't just stay barefoot in the snow.

She placed one freezing foot in front of the other. The ground had evened out, so she couldn't judge direction based on the incline of the hill.

The problem was, she didn't know if she was getting closer to the house, or farther away.

Another problem was that her feet were starting to burn, and feel like what she thought frostbite was like.

What the hell was she doing out here with no shoes? Being her damn reckless, impulsive self. But ultimately just running from her problems.

What the hell was she really doing up here in the north anyways? It's not like they didn't have plenty of temptation just waiting for her as soon as she got back. Who honestly would ever believe she was better?

She couldn't even find the way back to her own house. She might die out in this cold, and nobody would know for days, maybe even weeks.

"Help!" she screamed into the night. "HELP!"

Virginia wouldn't go out like this. She took off her fleece pajama top, gripping the collar with her numb hands. The wind reminded her of how awful it would be without a top, but her feet were killing her.

She bit the center hard, pulling at the fabric in either direction. With renewed vigor, she ripped the shirt in half. She wrapped one half around one foot, groping in the dark for where her own body was. She leaned on the tree for support, as she wrapped the other foot, as well.

Her ears stung. She couldn't stop shaking. But she would find her house. And if someone were in there waiting, there would be hell to pay.

Virginia took a slow step forward. The wrapping stayed on, though she could still feel the cold through it. Her appendages were numb. Her bare back, neck, and shoulders were rebelling against the chill night air, but there was nothing that could be done about it.

But then a whirring sound, an engine, a snowmobile. Headlights flashed in the distance, growing closer, the sound getting louder.

"HELP!" screamed Virginia. The fear was gone from her voice, replaced with a calm understanding of how dire her situation was.

The headlights slowed, turned mostly toward Virginia, then sped up.

Virginia waved her hands. As the light approached, she could see Sage's helmet and ski mask, her thick jacket and gloves manning the controls at the driver's seat.

As Sage approached, she slowed, taking in the scene. She pulled off her helmet and ski mask, hopping off the snowmobile with the engine still running.

"What are you doing out here?" Sage ran her fingers through her messy hair.

Virginia looked around the scene. She was naked from the waist up, her perky young breasts challenging the night with their pink spear tips.

There were drops of blood, and broken glass in the snow. Her side table lamp lay in a broken heap.

"I don't know." A sudden wave of shame overcame Virginia. She felt like flushing, but her body couldn't spare the heat.

"Do you want me to walk you back to your place?" Sage took a step closer.

Virginia shook her head fiercely. "I can't go back. There's someone in the house."

"Oh," Sage said. "Okay. Why don't you hop on my back?" It was a statement that sounded like a question. She maneuvered to where Virginia stood, shaking. She lifted one of her arms over her shoulder, muscling her back into the rest of the poor girl's body.

Virginia flopped onto Sage like a rag doll, shaking. She did not even hold on.

Sage held on to Virginia's arm with one hand, her other bent behind her back to support her weight. "Hold on, we'll be back at my place in a minute."

She lifted her powerful leg over the snowmobile, took her jacket off, and wrapped it around Virginia. She fit the ski mask over Virginia's face.

With Virginia firmly seated behind her, Sage grabbed her hands and made her hold on. Then she revved the engine, and spun in a half circle around the tree.

Sage steadily navigated through the trees. It could as easily have been a motorboat carving through water in the darkness, save the freezing blast of air cutting through her fabric like an icepick breaking up the lake.

Virginia hurt everywhere. She lost track of the passage of time with the pain, the lack of sleep, and the biting wind demanding her attention instead. They reached the lights of a small cottage.

Sage killed the engine, reached behind her, and hefted Virginia onto her back. Then she disembarked, taking deliberate, strong steps up a shoveled walkway. At the doorway, she lowered one hand to twist the knob, and carried Virginia inside.

As they entered, Denzel hopped up at them, barking much louder than usual.

The cottage was warm, but the heat stung Virginia's ears, fingers, and toes.

"You want to tell me what happened out there?" Sage set Virginia down, and stood back, evaluating the other woman.

Virginia rubbed what felt like a set of bruised knuckles. She swallowed, her mind racing. "I don't know."

"Come here." Sage took Virginia's hand, pulling her into the house.

"Oww..." Virginia stumbled forward. She looked up, pathetically. "I can't."

"Well you have to." Sage unzipped the jacket, sliding it off Virginia's shoulders. She turned away, reversing until Virginia was on her back once again. Then she steered her way to the bathroom, set Virginia on the sink counter, and ran a bath.

Sage turned to Virginia, locking into her gaze. "You're not thinking clearly right now. You need to get in the bath, because you might have frostbite. Do you think you can do that by yourself? Or do you want my help?"

Virginia tried to take a deep breath, but she was overwhelmed with emotion. "I think I can do it." She slid off the counter, and her sensitive feet gave way. She fell into Sage with all her weight.

Sage instinctually brought her arms up, catching Virginia. The two women looked at each other, their faces almost touching.

"Sorry," Virginia offered. She was too weak to move anymore, but at this moment she didn't want to. Her pain faded, her heart beating more rapidly. Her bare breasts pushed into Sage's bosom.

Outside the door, Denzel yipped softly.

Sage shouldered Virginia's weight. She reached her hands down Virginia's back, slipping her pajama pants down to her toes.

Virginia leaned in to the unintentional embrace, her lips brushing Sage's neck.

Sage lifted both hands under Virginia's butt and lifted her up. The last of the torn shirt fabric slid off her feet.

Virginia gasped in surprise, her arms holding Sage tighter.

Sage took two strides, then lowered Virginia into the bath.

"No, no, no!" Virginia scrambled. "It's too hot!"

Sage held onto her with firm, but gentle arms. "Whoa there, calm down. It's not hot at all. It's barely even warm."

Virginia struggled against the grip, her feet uselessly kicking against the slippery bathtub. "It hurts so much. I can't." She saw now that the ends of her feet were bright red, especially ringed at the toes.

Sage lowered her body to crouch by the bathtub, which caused Virginia, who was relying on her for support, to dip into the tub completely.

Sage leaned in and twisted the faucet handle. "This is the only way. I'm going to add some hot water, a little at a time. I need you to be brave, okay?"

Virginia nodded, her lips trembling. Surges of pain rushed through her body, as she shook violently.

Denzel scratched at the door, yipping, and yowling.

Sage hopped up to her feet, and opened the door.

Before it was open all the way, Denzel nosed through the crack, squeezing his body inside. He ran to the bath, and jumped up, setting his paws on the rim. His cute pink tongue dipped out of his mouth.

Virginia smiled. She lifted a wet hand, and scratched him behind the ears, drawing down to his cheeks and chin. She hiccupped in a few deep breaths.

Sage flicked on an electric heat lamp, which blew warm air from a glowing red coil mounted into the ceiling. "He wouldn't stop barking. I thought maybe it was a deer, or some big animal at first. But he just hopped up at the door, yelling his cute little head off."

She kneeled down, her hand running through Denzel's hind fur. "You have a special bond with Bartleby. I don't know how he knew you were in trouble, but he did."

Sage looked the dog over, her eyes lost in wonder. "I don't even know how he found you in the first place."

She looked up at Virginia. "But he did. He escaped from here, and found his way to a house he's never been to before."

Denzel hopped into Sage's lap, smashing his soft head into her stomach.

She laughed

Virginia dropped both her stinging hands into the tub. She was starting to get her sense of feeling back. The warm water slowly heating the bath was a welcome reprieve to an otherwise awkward evening.

She looked from Denzel, to Sage. "Maybe he's not what you think he is."

9

Coming Clean

Virginia tried to see the reflection of her eyes in the foggy mirror. She leaned in, her naked pelvis touching the warm marble. The heat lamp in Sage's bathroom felt amazing, working its magic all the way into her deep tissues, massaging her bones. How this tiny little hunting cabin could have such a modern amenity in it was beyond her comprehension.

But despite the haphazard architecture and lack of Feng Shui, or anything resembling design for that matter, there was an appeal to the practical nature of everything present. A purpose-driven home, with a seemingly purposeless owner.

Sage and Denzel had stepped outside to give Virginia some privacy, which having spent twenty minutes next to her in the bathtub while she was lying there naked, seemed more of a social courtesy.

She gave up on the mirror, too clouded in steam to get a visual. She couldn't bring herself to wipe it off because she knew what a chore it would be to clean in the morning, and she doubted that Sage was much of a cleaner. One look around the bathroom would confirm that.

Virginia slipped into a pair of fresh jogging shorts, and a tee shirt that Sage had left for her. Her hand cramped with pain when she pulled at the elastic, and shook as she put it through the shirtsleeve. She opened the bathroom door, letting out a cloud of steam to announce her grand entrance.

Sage sat in a rocking chair, a pistol in each hand.

Virginia's easy glide halted. She squirmed, taking in a room filled with hunting trophies, huge, glossy fish mounted on placards, and an old-school typewriter.

Denzel leapt from Sage's lap, running to lap up the little dew droplets still lingering on Virginia's ankles.

"You feeling better?" Sage lifted her head. She was either lost in thought, or dozing off while holding a pair of guns.

Virginia nodded. "Are those real?"

Sage waited for the punch line. "Don't you think I'm a little old to be playing Cowboys and Indians?"

Now it was Virginia who waited.

"Of course they're real. You said there was someone at your house." Sage yawned. "Here, this one's for you." She let go of the handle, and offered the gun, barrel now tilted up at the ceiling.

Virginia lifted her hands apologetically. "I don't know. Maybe it was a dream. I really thought I heard someone... saw something strange."

Sage nodded. "Maybe I freaked you out with my story." She looked at the larger of the guns, still pointed at the door. "I might still be a little freaked out myself."

"Can I ask you for a favor?" Virginia wiped her wet hair behind one ear. "Do you mind?" she motioned toward the guns.

Sage set the guns down on a wooden table, next to a lamp that had a tacky iron duck for a base, and a piece of fabric that might have been from when settlers first discovered this place, as a makeshift tablecloth.

"I just wanted to give you a hug," Virginia closed the distance, standing in front of Sage. "You really saved me out there tonight."

Sage looked up at Virginia. The shorts and tee were too big, but the baggy look only exacerbated her youthful beauty. She stood up slowly, a few inches taller than Virginia at her full height.

She raised up her hands like an apathetic prophet blessing a minion.

Virginia slipped herself under Sage's arms, wrapping her in a heartfelt embrace. She rested her head on Sage's chest. As she held on, Sage draped her arms over Virginia, hugging her back.

Virginia nuzzled her head into the soft space just below Sage's collarbone.

Sage took a step back, lifting her arms off Virginia. "I can't do this."

Virginia fell forward a step, catching herself. "I'm so sorry, I wasn't trying to offend you."

Sage shot her a questioning look. "No, I'm not offended. I'll be honest; it's quite the opposite. I find you attractive. I thought you understood I liked women when I told you that story."

Virginia locked in to Sage's eyes. "I absolutely understood that. I think I've been the one screwing up my subtle hints."

"Like what?" Sage asked.

Virginia stepped in, her triangular jawline aligning with Sage's more masculine features. Their lips grazed, but she applied pressure, adding a dash of tongue brush for effect.

"Like that."

Sage's pupil's widened. Had she really not caught on this entire time?

Now Sage leaned in, her lips catching Virginia's like prey. She brought her hands up again, reaching behind Virginia's back, this time pulling her in close.

Virginia let herself be taken, her eyelashes fluttering as she submitted to the dominant woman. She kissed back soft, and sweet. She was thankful to have borrowed Sage's mouthwash, her breath now hinted at cinnamon, cloves, and vanilla.

Sage offered her tongue, and Virginia gladly accepted. They locked onto each other, passionately kissing, groping, finding.

Virginia pulled back, and took a deep breath. Her eyes flashed around the room. "Why don't you have a bed?"

Sage nodded up, behind her.

Virginia followed her gaze. A metal spiral staircase cut into a little loft just below the roof.

Sage lowered her mouth, kissing Virginia's neck, tracing it up to the ear, where she gently nibbled.

Virginia smiled, her mouth opening as Sage pushed in. It had been way too long. She was ready.

"Could we go up?" she gasped as Sage lifted a strong hand up the inside of her tee shirt, finding a sensitive area at the small of her back that longed for more touch.

Sage dipped her hand down into the elastic of Virginia's shorts, running her fingers down the curvature of her lower half. The shorts slid to Virginia's ankles, exposing her hairless pelvis.

Sage ran the back of her hand up the front of Virginia, lingering at the seam.

Virginia leaned in, her breath coming to her in short bursts. "I want you so bad," she whispered.

"I want you so badly," Sage whispered back.

She shared a quick glance, and the two women giggled like they were kids again.

"I want you so badly," Virginia announced, smiling.

Sage nodded, removing her shirt. Now she was topless, and Virginia was bottomless, like a mismatched pair. She held out her hand, taking Virginia's as she walked toward the tight staircase.

They wound their way around the central pillar, arriving at a disheveled but homey cove at the top. It was much warmer up here, which made sense because there wasn't much room between the soft mattress and the triangular corner of the roof as it reached its peak here.

Sage lay down on her back, her head landing in the soft cushions. She reached under the pillow, and pulled out a hunting knife, tossing it with a loud thud to the wooden planks next to the bed.

Virginia rolled on top, her legs straddling, her bald eagle spread. She leaned down and kissed Sage fervently, her desire coming through in breathy, guttural noises.

Tiny footprints plinked on the metal stairs below, little claws tapping as they hopped up stair by stair.

Both women turned their heads to see two black ears pop up into the attic, followed by an adorable fuzzy black head, with one pink tongue hanging out of its mouth. They giggled in harmony.

Sage realigned, eagerly kissing Virginia's breasts through her shirt.

Denzel bounded across the soft covers, and eagerly licked Virginia's forearms, which held her weight.

Virginia giggled again. "Denzel, you're not invited to this party."

Sage continued shuffling her body down the bed. Her mouth found the exposed side of Virginia, under the ribs. She kissed inch by inch down to Virginia's sexy ridge of muscle at her waistline, defined by hours of lonely yoga.

"Yes," Virginia whispered, closing her eyes.

Sage planted a trail of gentle kisses, wet and warm, until she reached the center. She kissed the top, the sides, the middle. Then she ran her tongue from the base, upwards.

Virginia's shoulders slouched, her face buried in the cushions. "Oh my god, that feels so good. Don't stop!"

Sage was one step ahead of her, caressing Virginia's lips inside and out with her soft tongue, French kissing the sensitive button at the top of the crease. She reached up and grabbed Virginia's ass, bringing her hips down, deeper into her mouth, pushing Sage's head firmly back into the bed.

Virginia grabbed for the sheets, digging her fingers into the mattress. "Oh my god, oh my god, oh my god." She ignored the pain from her battered right hand as it squeezed tighter.

Sage worked into a frenzied rhythm, devouring Virginia.

Virginia thrust her hips forward again, and again, and again. Her eyes popped open when she felt a warm, wet tongue licking the cuts on her knuckles.

Denzel lapped at the back of Virginia's hand, maintaining eye contact.

"Stop," Virginia hissed.

Sage stopped.

Denzel continued.

"No, no, no!" Virginia cried. "More please! Denzel stop."

Sage continued where she left off.

Virginia closed her eyes and rested her forehead against the wall.

Denzel continued where he left off.

Virginia tried to put it out of her mind, which was easy as it went blank. She tried to focus on her breathing, but she couldn't hold it if she tried.

Sage reached into her shorts to touch herself. She mimicked the pattern of motion as she rocked Virginia back and forth, her other hand clutching Virginia's hip.

Virginia relaxed into the easy rocking, the muscles from her lower back all the way down through her butt cheeks twanging as she started to clamp up.

Her pleasure was all Sage needed to make short work of herself. She moaned, muffled by her mouth cupped around Virginia.

That sent Virginia over the edge, filling the room with the sounds of her pleasure as chills went down her neck, and spine. She pushed her hips forward in one final thrust, using the last of her energy.

Sage kissed her one more time; sending ripples of aftershock to Virginia's lower half. Then she pulled herself out from underneath, and crawled up beside, snuggling in. She wrapped her hand around Virginia's back.

"That was amazing, thank you." Virginia mumbled into the pillow. "I want you to feel good, too."

"I already took care of that," Sage took a deep breath, sighing.

"Okay," Virginia paused. "I'm sorry I can't open my eyes. I want to." She breathed deeply into the pillow, nodding off.

Sage smiled. "It's not a problem."

Soft greyish blue light slowly filled the room, as it reflected the sunrise off the morning snow outside the windows of the cabin.

Sage rolled onto her side, lifting herself to her knees. She pulled two makeshift black fabric curtains closed along a bar positioned above the edge of the loft.

Virginia startled herself awake. She blinked her eyes and watched Sage close the curtains. She hadn't noticed them, or almost any of the loft when she first crept up. It had been a long night.

Sage lay down next to her once more.

Denzel softly padded around in circles, before settling at their feet.

Virginia squeezed into the crook of Sage's arm. Her head nestled comfortably between Sage's breast and chin. Something tugged at the back of her brain, wondering if the front door was locked, but she couldn't keep up with the thought as darkness washed over her.

10

Overanalyzing

Virginia opened her eyes slowly. The smell of bacon pooled in the loft where she lay cozily. Denzel still slept at her feet, his head pressed into her calves.

She looked down at herself. There were no covers on her body. Her bare torso gleamed golden in the reflected light. Of all the issues she had, worrying about her beauty was not one of them. True, she spent a lot of time thinking about makeup, wardrobe, shoes, and style because it was part of the business. But she knew that deep down, underneath all the glitz and glamor, she had a body to be envied.

It was nice to see it naked again, and not have to worry about covering up in layers of clothing, and blankets before the chill set in. She would have to ask Sage about the insulation in her house.

Virginia yawned, running her hands up the borrowed tee shirt until she reached her breasts. She let them rest there, feeling good. It was nice to have someone experienced like Sage at the helm last night. Virginia was usually pretty quick compared to most, but her orgasm was eager for release. It had been way too long since she had been with anyone other than her rabbit vibrator, and her left hand.

She rolled over, and spotted the hunting knife lying on the wooden planks of the attic. A knife that big under your pillow seemed like overkill, but Sage was still recovering from some intense trauma. She couldn't imagine, although she did try to do the math.

If Sage had inherited Denzel's mama, who didn't seem to be around, then it had to have take place in the last twenty human years, give or take. Could a dog possibly live longer than twenty years? Probably not.

Additionally, Sage had been childhood friends and then sweethearts with the girl. So were they teens, or adults when all this went down? Judging from her age, that could have been as long as twenty-five years ago, possibly longer. But then that would mean Virginia's cabin had been vacant for longer than she was alive.

Creepy. No wonder it seemed off.

Downstairs, something metal clanged in quick succession. Was it part of Sage's cooking process, or a signal that breakfast was ready?

Virginia stood up, and looked around the area, recalling that her shorts had come off downstairs.

Denzel hopped up to his feet, charging her playfully. He leapt up onto his back legs, pawing at her, and licking her knees.

Virginia went to the metal spiral staircase, exposed. It was like a walk of shame before she'd even left the house.

Denzel's clawed feet tapped the metal loudly, announcing them both as they descended.

Sage stood at the base of the staircase, hands on her hips, spatula in one hand. Her mouth was upturned, which though it lacked warmth, appeared to be a smile.

"Good morning," heat rushed through Virginia's chest to her face. She was not ashamed of her naked lower half, but keenly aware of the sharp contrast to the fully clothed Sage.

Sage nodded. "I made some breakfast." She turned her back, and walked into the kitchen section, which was one corner of the living room. The house appeared much smaller in the daylight, as it was basically a studio apartment with one door to the bathroom, one door that led outside, and the loft.

Virginia was quick to pick up on the curt nature of Sage's actions, the quick dip of her head, the smile that lifted the mouth, but not the cheeks. Had she done something to offend her? Or was Sage really not good around other people?

"Thank you again for last night," Virginia said softly. She considered her words carefully. "For everything. You saved me. And then you went above and beyond."

Sage turned to face her, allowing a quick upturn of the head in recognition.

"Thank you," Virginia reiterated. "I can walk home if it's a hassle having me here."

Sage narrowed her eyes. "You can go, if you want."

Virginia raised her hands peaceably, trying to read her. "Okay."

Sage picked up two plates, filled with steaming food. "If you're hungry, breakfast is ready."

Virginia nodded, holding her breath.

Sage brought the plates out into the living room, handing one to Virginia, along with a fork. There was no dining room table, so she set hers next to the rocking chair.

Virginia rested her naked bottom across from her in a chair that was either an antique in desperate need of care, or something that would be firewood before the winter let up. Speaking of which, she saw that a flurry of snow was falling.

So much for spring.

Virginia poked at her plate. Eggs, strips of meat, and short, fat, pancakes with syrup drizzled over the butter.

"You don't eat much?" Sage breathed out steam, talking around a chunk of meat she cooled in her jaw.

Virginia shot a cool gaze back up at her. "I love food. But I'm more of a pescetarian. I'm also gluten free."

Sage nodded, cutting into her pancakes with the dull side of her fork. "Bummer."

"I hope you don't think I'm judging you for what you eat," Virginia fixed her gaze on Sage.

"Nope," Sage took a big bite of pancake. "I eat food when I'm hungry. Then when I'm full I stop eating."

"Okay," Virginia was struggling. She wanted the conversation to go well, but something was off. "I'm just saying it's not because I'm self-righteous. I know my body doesn't do well with wheat, or red meat. It's totally not a criticism of what you eat."

Sage took another big bit of pancake, watching Virginia struggle. It was hard to tell if she was amused, or pissed off. It seemed like both.

Virginia picked at her eggs, taking small bites.

They ate quietly. Outside, the glistening snow came faster, the wind blowing it sideways now. But it was easier to see sunlight from Sage's house, and the day was surprisingly bright. The cabin was cozy, and warm, even with no lights on.

Sage stood up, holding her empty plate.

"Sorry, I didn't finish." Virginia offered her plate of pancakes, and meat. The egg was mostly picked clean.

Sage accepted the plate, setting it on the floor of the kitchen.

Denzel's ears perked up, and he ran to inspect this new delicacy. He wolfed down the sausage, then crunched into the bacon.

Virginia took this opportunity to find the shorts that Sage had loaned her last night, and slip them on.

Sage washed the dishes, then returned to her seat in the chair. She looked at Virginia.

Virginia suddenly felt a chill. She brought her feet up into the chair, holding her legs with her arms. "Do you think... Bartleby heard me last night?"

Sage grinned, a gleam in her eye.

Virginia blushed. "I mean when I was stuck outside. Before I came over."

Sage considered it, bobbing her head from side to side. "Dogs do have better hearing than we do."

"I'm thankful…" Denzel leapt up into Virginia's lap, smashing into her breasts as he brought his greasy maw toward her neck. His tongue darted in and out, sneaking in to her cheeks.

"Yes, you," Virginia cooed. "I'm very grateful. Thank you for knowing I needed help. It's like you're a being of light, and goodness." She scratched behind his ears, working her way down his furry body.

She peered around his face, still licking her, and caught Sage's eye. "What I'm trying to say is, don't you think it's strange he could sneak out of here and find my house? And then last night, he knew I needed help?"

Sage stared blankly back.

Virginia wiped grease and slobber from her neck, and cheeks. "He's like a rescue dog, but so much more than that. I think he brought us together for a reason."

Sage wasn't saying anything. Danger.

"I'm not saying we're like a couple or anything, but you know, we keep running into each other." Virginia rested her chin on Denzel's head, as he gently rubbed his wet nose on her. She narrowed her eyes. "You don't think that's odd?"

Sage reached for the bottle of whiskey next to her. She uncapped it, and drank.

"I'm not trying to make a big deal out of this," Virginia swept her hand across the open space. "I was just thinking that maybe Denzel," she looked down. "Maybe he's a reincarnated soul, or something."

She looked at Sage, but she still couldn't get a read on her. "I don't necessarily believe in stuff like that, but isn't it strange?"

Sage took another swig of whiskey, and then capped the bottle. "I have a lot of work to do today." She stood up, and stretched.

"Totally," Virginia realized she was talking too fast, and sounded like a kook.

Sage walked across the space to a dresser, digging out pants, socks, a sweater, and a spare coat. "It's not far to your house, but I don't know if you could find it in this weather." She tossed the clothes on the table next to Virginia.

Maybe Virginia had misread Sage. Maybe Sage wasn't feeling it. Or maybe she wasn't as lonely as she seemed. She might even have a girlfriend living somewhere in the woods. Regardless, she could take a hint.

Virginia gently brushed Denzel to the warm spot in the chair, then picked up the spare clothes, and went to the bathroom to change. Her mind started spinning, trying to remember everything she said last night. Had she offended Sage?

This is why you can't do relationships Virginia. You're a mess. You're already overanalyzing and you haven't left her house yet.

She shook her head, telling the mirror 'no.'

Virginia slipped into the winter gear, way too warm for the house. When she stepped out of the bathroom, Sage was changed already, her ski mask rolled up into a beanie.

Sage handed Virginia a spare pare of boots, heavy and far too big.

It was insinuated that Sage would provide a ride, but Virginia wanted to walk. That being said, she was positive she would be lost even without the snowfall, so she grudgingly accepted the implied ride.

She plopped her feet into the boots, and followed Sage outside.

Sage pulled the ripcord on the snowmobile, and it thrummed.

"I hope you don't think I'm a weirdo." Virginia climbed behind Sage on the snowmobile, holding on.

"You are a weirdo." Sage shrugged through her bulky jacket. "We're all weirdoes when people get to know us, right?" She thrummed the engine, starting slowly, but getting to speed fast.

They blew through the snowfall, the forest white, and quiet, save the roar of their machine. It was only a few minutes before they were at Virginia's cabin. Sage slowed the snowmobile, pausing it as she sidled up to the snow bank demarcating Virginia's yard.

Virginia took a few clumsy steps dismounting, the oversized boots not helping. "Thank you. I'll get your stuff back to you soon." She walked up the fresh snow toward her entryway.

"Let me know if you see any reincarnated spirits," Sage called after her.

Virginia opened the unlocked door. "It's fine," she called back.

A loud bang from inside the house sent Virginia scuttling backwards, her hands flying up to protect her face.

Sage dismounted the snowmobile, a pistol now in her hand. She walked between Virginia, and the door. Then she crept forward, quietly pushing her way into the house, gun first.

Virginia was right behind Sage, her hand resting on the back of her coat. Her eyes widened as she braced herself for the all too familiar, yet unnatural tingling.

11

Worthy

Virginia held her breath. This was the proof she was looking for: now Sage had to believe in ghosts. On the other hand, she wasn't going to spend another minute in a cabin where the dead roamed, so this would close down her rehab experiment. That wasn't such a terrible thing; she had gone one hundred seventeen days without a pick-me-up. Not that anyone was counting.

Despite her oversized boots, Sage moved quietly, steadily, like a beast of prey. Her calculated motion was in direct contrast to Virginia's clomping, squeaking, footsteps.

Sage shot a warning glance behind her, but her face softened when she saw the terror in Virginia's eyes. She lifted the gun with both hands, edging her shoulder to the corner of the door. She was a natural, actually. She looked like she belonged in whatever action movie their real lives were playing out.

In a heartbeat, Sage whipped around through the kitchen door, her gun pointed chest-level.

Virginia crept up behind her, standing on her toes to see over Sage's shoulder.

In the kitchen an older, balding man with few teeth smiled at them, continuing to unpack groceries out of a brown paper bag.

"Ernie? What are you doing here?" Sage demanded.

"Umm," Virginia put her hand on Sage's shoulder. "He delivers my groceries."

Sage lowered the gun, holstering it. "Sorry. Would you like a hand?"

"Sure," Ernie nodded to the bags still on the floor. "I brought some extra cans of dog food this week. Curtis said you picked some up a few days ago."

Sage shot a glance back at Virginia that lacked definition, but appeared to blend relief with annoyance. "Ernie where's your snowmobile?"

Ernie laughed a broken, wheezy rasp. "On a breezy day like this? I skied here." He peeked out to where the snow was still bundling down from the sky. "Thought I might trek back to Blueberry Hill before I head home."

Sage reached in and pulled out a steak, in a plastic-wrapped Styrofoam tray. She cast an accusatory glance at Virginia.

Virginia looked from the steak, to Ernie.

Ernie chuckled. "I know, I know. You told me no more steak. But everyone loves a good steak. I'll cook it for you if you don't know how."

Virginia sighed, smiling. "No thank you, Ernie. I still don't eat steak, no matter how well it's cooked. It's just not my preference." She winked at Sage. "Would you like a nice steak?"

Sage pulled out a box of rice crackers, inspecting them. "Nope. I don't eat farm-raised meats. Only eat what I kill."

Virginia wasn't expecting that. But now Sage's irritation over breakfast made more sense: it wasn't just that Virginia didn't eat what Sage cooked; it was that she was rejecting Sage's lifestyle. But there had to be more than that; Sage was irritated before breakfast.

Virginia picked up the wrapped steak from the counter, handing it to Ernie. "Why don't you take this, and cook it for yourself? Just tell me how it turns out, and we'll call it good."

Ernie held the steak, looking at Virginia thoughtfully.

Virginia rested her hand on Ernie's shoulder. "Seeing you happy would make me happy."

Ernie smiled, revealing three lower front teeth hiding in his expansive brown gums. "Are you sure you don't want some cigarettes, or real coffee out here?"

Virginia shook her head. "Trust me, I want those things very much. But I can't push my luck."

Ernie narrowed his eyes, trying to comprehend. "Cause they're bad for your skin?"

Virginia nodded. "Something like that, yes."

He beamed. "You do have very pretty skin."

"Thank you."

"Yes," Sage chimed in. "Thank you, Ernie."

"Have a safe ski trek," Virginia added, in case he didn't pick up on the first social cue.

Ernie fumbled in his pockets for a moment, checking his pants, his jacket, his shirt. "Welcome. Just radio if you need anything in particular. Otherwise I'll just stick to the list." He wrapped the steak up in an empty brown bag, and walked to the front door. "Really coming down now, isn't it?" He popped his boots on, and disappeared into the flurry.

Virginia looked at Sage. Her skin was fine, flawless. Her rosy red cheeks added a summer glow to her otherwise pale and delicate, yet strong features. She appeared prettier every time Virginia looked at her. But what was inside that head of hers?

"You eat a lot of vegetables. And fruit." Sage casually looked at the rainbow display on the kitchen counter.

"I do," Virginia stepped toward Sage. "I really enjoyed last night, even in spite of all the…"

Sage shifted her weight.

"You know – what happened. I'm not usually like that." Virginia tried to read her for a sign, for anything.

Sage turned her shoulders to face her head on, her arms crossed. "What are you usually like?"

Virginia delicately rested her hands on Sage's arms, slowly pulling them apart. "That's a good question. I'm kind of reinventing myself right now."

Sage hesitantly let herself be moved. "Isn't that what you do for a living?"

"That's a good point." Virginia laid her head on Sage's chest. She brought a hand down on her collarbone, tracing the line with her finger. "I haven't had it as easy as everyone assumes."

Sage held firm. "I don't assume anyone has it easy."

Virginia tilted her head back, looking up, and into Sage's eyes. "That's one of the reasons I like you."

Sage shrugged Virginia off. "Maybe also because I'm the only other dyke out here."

Virginia stood up straight as Sage backed away. "What? No... that's what you think?" She shook her head. "No way."

"Look, I get it," Sage put her hands up. "You miss having some company, I'm the closest thing around. But come on. I'm at least ten years older than you, and you're perfect." She looked Virginia up and down. "Don't pretend it's anything more than what it is."

Virginia opened her mouth to say something, reaching her hand up for Sage.

Sage backed away another step. "You don't have to act around me."

"I'm not acting," Virginia managed, her voice a whisper.

Sage looked down at her boots. They were still wearing their winter gear inside the house. She brushed past Virginia, out the kitchen, to the front door.

"Wait!" Virginia called. She walked to the kitchen entrance, looking at the front door.

Sage hesitated, waiting for her to say something. Then she opened the door, and disappeared into the whirling snow.

Virginia walked to the door. She watched the outline of Sage, as she grew faint. What could she say? She kicked off the oversized boots, threw the jacket into the corner, and tore off the sweater.

She swatted at stray snowflakes as they blew inside. "Stupid snow."

She slammed the door, storming to the living room. "Stupid cabin."

She walked into the bathroom, looking at her reflection. It was leaking spiteful tears. "Stupid you." She opened the medicine cabinet. Still bare.

Then she slammed the mirror shut, sending sprinkles of broken glass into the sink bowl. Something stung her feet. She looked down to see a few little shards had broken her skin.

Virginia took a wide step out the door, away from the mess. She sat down in the hallway, lifting her foot towards her face. "Stupid, stupid." She held her calf with one hand, and carefully picked the stray pieces out of her skin. Little droplets of blood pooled at the exit wounds.

She held the broken bits in one palm, pushing herself to her feet with the other. She walked to the kitchen, tossing the shards into the trash. Outside, the wind was swirling flurries of snow in every direction. It was crazy to think that Ernie was out there somewhere on his skis, hopefully alive and well. On that note hopefully stupid Sage made it home safe, too.

Okay, Virginia. Maybe it's time to chill out.

She opened the fridge, hoping to find something good to snort, but it was just food. Same with the cabinets: crackers, peanut butter, pasta. No Adderall. No Vikodin. No Xanax.

Fucking past Virginia was so damn thorough with this house. Nothing. No drugs. Nothing that even resembles drugs. Not even coffee. Not even cocaine.

She sat on the ground. Her feet were cold. She needed her fuzzy slippers. Something soft. She needed a hug. She needed someone to tell her that things were okay, that she was nailing this recovery thing.

Virginia rocked back and forth. What a lie. The only reason she wasn't back in the game was because there was no game up here. The second she set foot back in LA, the party would start right back up where she left off. And then fuck that uppity bitch Sage. What was she so mad about anyways? Virginia didn't even do anything yet. Other than steal her dog, accidentally. And smash a lamp on a tree, accidentally.

Was it happening again? Maybe Virginia didn't need drugs to be a sloppy mess. Maybe she was just a natural. Why fight the urge to get crazy when she already was crazy?

Breathe, Virginia.

She leaned back against the cabinet.

This was the big top loop of the spiral. This is when things started to get out of hand. It was time to check in, instead of checking out.

I love myself.

Not yet, but she was working on that part.

I am a beautiful human being.

Outwardly, obviously. Inwardly, she was working on that part, too.

I am worthy of being loved.

Everyone is worthy of being loved. Even the crazy ones. The wild ones. The bad ones. The broken ones. The ones who were a mix of all those unlovable traits.

It doesn't mean that everyone in the world is going to love you, or has to love you. It means that you're worthy of their love, if they choose to make that investment. So ultimately, it was Sage who was missing out by choosing to turn her back on this beautiful mess.

There was one person in this world that loved Virginia unconditionally, and Denzel wasn't even technically a person. Virginia realized she truly loved Denzel back.

Virginia walked to the front door, and locked it. She wasn't going to risk another night sleeping in a haunted house because she wanted to believe in affirmations, and love conquering all.

12

Captured

Virginia woke with a start.

The wind howled past the cold panes, whipping the relentless snow into clumps on the sills. It hadn't stopped since this morning.

Footsteps downstairs. Faint, but recognizable.

A chill spiraled down Virginia's back, despite the heat trapped inside the nest of blankets.

This time, she was ready. She slid a pillow into her cozy spot, and tucked the blankets back down the bed. She picked her phone up off the side table, then slipped down the opposite side, away from the door. The door was already ajar, and she left the hallway light on.

Virginia flicked the phone into camera mode, and began to videotape whatever was happening. She needed it, if only to play it for herself the next day to prove that she wasn't making this up.

But the footsteps were audible, and coming closer. Hopefully the camera was picking this up. But that didn't bring her any comfort right now.

Why are you filming this, idiot? Grab a weapon!

And do what with a weapon? What good did it do Sage to have all those guns, and knives lying around? She was still a wreck of a human. She had no idea what she was missing out on.

Footsteps walking up the stairs.

Virginia lay flat against the ground, the camera edge of her phone peeking around the bed, while she watched the screen. Her heart was pounding so hard she could feel it thumping the floor.

Footsteps at the top landing. And then a pair of boots landed toe first outside her door. Quietly. Creeping. Something dark filled the crack of the door, a jacket, snow pants. They were looking in.

Could they see the bed?

Could they see the camera?

Virginia held her breath. Who the fuck would be here now? Nobody else had a key. Was it the same person as the other night? Was it Ernie? Or Sage?

Too many questions. She tried to steady her shaking hand, pressed against the floor, and leaned against the bed corner.

The light seeped in from the hallway once again. The figure blocking the light moved on. The footsteps continued softly down the hall.

Virginia had studied stage combat. She knew about martial arts, self-defense, and how to make a weapon look very threatening. But something told her this wasn't going to help her now, far away from everyone and everything. Whatever this dark presence was, it wasn't going to scare easily.

It was too quiet.

The footsteps stopped. Now there was only the sound of Virginia's heart beating too fast. Her breaths coming in spurts.

Tomorrow, she would leave this cabin, and never come back. This little experiment had run its course. Whatever the future might hold, she had a good run of being alone, and sober.

The footsteps returned, coming back down the hall toward her bedroom. But they passed by, sneaking down the stairs.

Virginia picked up her phone, leaving the camera recording. She didn't have a face, only a silhouette. Someone tall, most likely a man judging by weight, and dress. Someone who knew how to get into a locked door without smashing it.

Was it worth sneaking out there only to die, for the satisfaction of knowing who was here?

Virginia picked up one foot, placing it a few inches in front of the other. She slowly repeated until she reached her open bedroom door. Not a creek.

Downstairs, it was quiet.

Virginia opened the door just wide enough to squeeze her head out. She slowly leaned out far enough to see down the hall, and down the staircase to part of the living room.

Nothing unusual.

With painstaking care, she hugged the wall, sliding the rest of her body out the bedroom door. Bare feet stepping gingerly on the cold wood floor, she made it to the top landing of the staircase, leaning over the rail to see the entire living room.

Nothing unusual.

Past the fireplace, down the short walk to the entryway she could see the lower corner of the front door. It was closed. Was it still locked?

Was whatever thing that was in her house right now already in here when she locked it?

She shivered involuntarily, backing away from the railing.

Maybe there was some secret room, or door in the house where someone, or something lived. Nightmare images from horror movies started filling her brain.

Was it the ghost of the daughter who was murdered? Was it Sage's father, back from the dead to reap the souls of the living?

Virginia crept back inside her bedroom, adjusting the door to where it had been before she messed with it. She resumed her spot laying behind the bed, setting up her phone to rest on the corner so she didn't have to hold it.

Adrenaline was pumping through her body. Lying down was excruciating. It was time to fight, flee, anything other than waiting.

She glanced at the screen of her phone: eighteen minutes and counting. She hadn't heard anything since the footsteps went downstairs – including the door opening, or closing. But why would someone break into the house just to scare her?

It's not like anyone was making a bid to buy this shithole cabin. Sage even said that everyone around knew that it was haunted. Unless… the cabin was haunted by someone real – someone still alive – someone who used to live here.

Supposedly the father was in jail for a double murder. Why had Sage never mentioned the mother? And without Sage testifying, could they even put the father in jail?

Virginia could hear the sound of her brain humming in overdrive. There were so many possibilities, and none of them were pleasant. As she bounced from one grim scenario to the next, she watched the time counter spin on her phone.

Whatever had been here was gone now. The pulsing in her body dimmed, the energy reserves sapped, the late hour taking its toll.

Her eyes stung. She closed them for a moment, just to get them back to normal.

It felt good. She closed them again.

She didn't recall falling asleep, but when she opened her eyes, the room was filled with bluish-grey morning light.

Virginia lifted her head off of her arm.

An arms length away, her phone lay face down on the ground. She stretched her sore arm, picking up the phone.

Dead.

Virginia shot to her feet. She hopped on the bed, reaching into the drawer for the charging cable.

Casting a backward glance at her door, Virginia plugged her phone into the wall. She set the phone down, and walked to the door, opening it slowly.

She walked into the hallway, opening every drawer, door, and cabinet she could find. She grabbed a baseball bat, gripping it in one hand. It was new, shiny wood, purchased solely because her agent Callie insisted that a single woman alone in the woods needed something, just in case.

Time to practice gratitude, Virginia.

Thank you for looking out for me, Callie.

Thank you for not giving up on me when everyone else did.

Thank you for trusting me. May I prove that you were right.

Virginia continued her search, walking down the stairs. The top floor would be virtually impossible for anyone to hide, let alone live in secrecy.

She looked around the open living room, sparsely furnished with the new couch she bought, and a couple of relics that came with the house. The gas fireplace was pumping out its usual pittance of warmth, but Virginia was flushed with excitement.

She checked the coat closet, which only had coats and winter gear inside.

The front door was still locked, although it didn't have the type of bolt that only locked from the inside. Anyone with a key, or a good lock pick set could get in.

Rounding the corner of the kitchen, Virginia clicked the light on, and opened the pantry. Nothing was out of place.

This was silly. When Denzel lived here, he would have known if someone were hiding in the house. He would have sniffed them out, like he did the raccoons.

Virginia picked a rice flour bagel out of the package, and popped it in the toaster. She got the Nutella from the cabinet, and the Italian butter from the fridge. It's impossible to track down stalker ghosts on an empty stomach. Science has proven that.

The toaster popped, and Virginia whipped her body toward the noise, gripping her baseball bat hard. She breathed a sigh of relief, then set the bat on the counter. She lathered the flavorless rice bagel with toppings, and plated it.

She took a bite of the bagel, savoring the chewy texture. Nothing compared to wheat, but eating that was too uncomfortable to bear. Her stomach thanked her for anything right now – she hadn't eaten since picking at yesterday's eggs at Sage's cabin.

Virginia hated fighting. It reminded her of childhood, poverty, being alienated from her family, shitty producers who demanded unreasonable things – the 'anythings' it takes to make it to the top.

She walked into the living room, smiling. What a journey it was to make it this far, into a cabin by herself, in a winter storm, in the middle of the woods. Was this why she had worked so many grueling hours, days, months? Only to have to confront her own demons after all?

Why couldn't you buy something to help get over it already? That's what the damn drugs, and drinks were for in the first place. What a vicious cycle.

She finished the first half of the bagel, and licked Nutella from her thumb. She slowly ascended the stairs, entering her bedroom. She walked to the nightstand where her phone was charging.

It could be that this entire ordeal was a figment of her imagination, her demons working their way out. She held down the power button and turned her phone on, looking out the window as the loading screen came on. Snow was breezing by, though the intensity, and wind had died down.

Virginia unlocked her phone, and tapped on her photo album. She clicked on the most recent movie. Good god, four plus hours of her hiding behind the bed. How much of that was wasted when the phone fell forward?

She turned the audio up to full blast, and played the recording.

Virginia closed her eyes. As the video played, she could hear the footsteps faintly.

It was real.

She opened her eyes, and set her bagel down. She realized her body unconsciously reverted to that primal state of fear from last night, her heart beating rapidly. She watched the silhouette on screen fill the frame of her door, then walk away. But when did the phone fall over? It must have happened after she was asleep.

Virginia scrolled along the video until it went dark, then backed up.

The boots were outside her door again. But this time, the door opened. The shadow filled the room, walking in slowly. The open door cast more light from the hallway, but the silhouetted face was still indistinguishable. The figure walked up to the bed, then directly in front of the phone camera.

A big thumb came into view, covering the camera lens, and the phone tilted down to the ground. Everything on screen went black. Then the sound of boots walking back out the door.

Virginia felt ice prickling her veins, her golden arm hairs standing on end. She set the bagel plate down with a shaking hand, her other hand clutching her phone. The baseball bat was downstairs on the kitchen counter.

13

Such Sweet Sorrow

Anxiety bubbled up in Virginia's body, manifesting itself as adrenaline, discomfort, and an upset stomach. Her mind raced into different possibilities with new outcomes, none of them pleasant.

One the one hand, her gut feeling was correct. This thing was scary, and real. On the other hand, why did it leave her alone? That was the worst part, not knowing what it was, or who it was, or what they wanted.

Regardless, it was time to go. Virginia crept out of the room, holding her phone to her chest. She snuck down the stairs, peering out the window. It was hard to see much through the flurry of snow blowing softly. She knew from experience it would be a huge risk trying to make it to town on her own.

She speed walked to the kitchen, trying to keep her footsteps quiet. It didn't matter that she already searched the house, and discovered she was alone. Her heart was pounding.

Virginia grabbed the baseball bat off the kitchen counter, and dashed back into the living room. She flicked on the radio, and it gave a mighty pop. Then, she picked up the microphone, and pressed the button. "Ernie? Ernie, can you hear me?"

She let go of the button, and it crackled with static. Did he even have his radio on? "Ernie? Are you there? Come in, Ernie."

Virginia inspected the spiral cord, making sure the microphone, and power plugs were in. She tugged at the cord at the back. Everything was mechanically sound.

The radio crackled, then Ernie's voice came in, "Ten-one, my dear. Over." It was choppy, but audible.

"Ernie, it's Virginia."

"Hey there, Beauty! Thanks so much for that steak, it was delicious. I saved you a bite, like I promised. Over."

"Ernie," Virginia tried to rein it in, but she could feel herself getting emotional. "I need to go. Now."

It was quiet on the other line. Then the static and, "Ten-four, my dear. Go where? Is everything okay?" He was wheezing into his microphone. "Is this about the situation? Over."

Virginia buzzed back. "No. I'm clean. It's not about that. I'll explain when you get here, if I can. But I need to go home, now. You can call Callie, and tell her it's an emergency."

Ernie took too long to respond. He was thinking about it too hard. This did sound bad, what else would he possibly think it was, than an addict having a meltdown and trying to use?

The crackle came through. "Are you sure? Do you want to take a day to think about it? Over."

"No, Ernie," Virginia tried to stay calm. Desperation wasn't going to sell her story. "I have to go now. If you can't come pick me up, I'm going to walk into town and hitchhike out of here if I have to."

"Hold on there, my dear. I'll come on out. It might take a little longer than usual: we got a few extra inches last night and this morning. Visibility is pretty low for riding around, but you hang on okay? I'll be out as quick as I can."

"Thank you, Ernie."

Virginia realized she was clutching the bat so hard, her bicep was hurting. She relaxed, shaking her arm out, rotating between clenching, and opening her hand.

Goodbye lake, and useless boat. Goodbye crazy blizzard.

She took a deep breath. She couldn't leave without saying goodbye to Denzel, even if that meant being the bigger woman, and confronting Sage. She also felt like she owed it to Sage to show her whatever she had captured on video – not to prove a point, but because Sage lived in the next cabin over.

Virginia went to the coat closet, and donned a warm jacket, and snow pants. She bundled up in a hat, mittens, and her thick boots. Then she picked up a plastic bag with Virginia's loaner clothes, and boots. She juggled the baseball bat to her other hand.

This shouldn't be hard in the daytime. She unlocked the door, and opened it, slowly.

The coast was clear, aside from the constant snowfall. Now or never – Ernie should be here in an hour, or so. Granted, he was always late, but she did say this was an emergency.

Virginia closed the door behind her, but left it unlocked, in case he did actually rush over. She circled the house, just for peace of mind, but nobody was hiding behind the walls. There weren't even any footprints other than hers.

She walked out to where her yard slumped over into what would be a dirt road in summer, or spring if it weren't still snowing so hard. From there it should be a straight shot up the hill to Sage's house. It was still early enough that the light was decent, despite the flurries, and the tall trees.

Virginia put one boot in front of the other, crunching into soft snow. She left a trail of deep imprints behind her. She stopped to catch her breath, as she cleared the top of the hill. Trying to exercise in the winter felt like mountain climbing, the air pierced her lungs, reminding her how much this place sucked.

Virginia followed the road as it twisted through the fir trees. Ahead, Sage's wood cabin was nestled under a layer of fresh snow, like a maple syrup logo. Sometimes the people and things around here were parodies of themselves. But there was something about Sage. Underneath all that pain was a unique woman. A beautiful woman. A damaged, emotionally unavailable woman.

Sage's snowmobile was parked outside her door. She was home alright, unless she was off killing a deer, or something. No, she was probably sitting in her chair, drinking whiskey and hanging out with Denzel. Supposedly she was a big deal writer, but when did she ever actually write?

Deep breath. Virginia would be on an airplane in a few hours, and Sage would just be a funny anecdote about dating in the north woods, to tell other girls at parties when she got back to LA. Back where people appreciated how Virginia was. Like seriously, was everyone up here except old Ernie blind?

Virginia walked toward the door, looking at the small staircase up to the stoop, mostly covered in snow. The winters had taken their toll on the wood, turning it brownish-green. Like the rest of the house it suffered from inattention to detail, and while it was probably structurally sound, it appeared rickety, and emotionally unavailable.

Knocking might be too obvious. What if Sage pulled a gun on her? What if she was still pissed about whatever she was originally pissed about? And what was she originally pissed about?

Sage said something about Virginia being perfect. Kind of like the other day when she mentioned that Virginia didn't know what it was like to lose people, or feel pain. Seemed like some victim mentality bullshit.

Virginia shuffled around the side of the house, slowly. Time for little miss Perfect to do some snooping. It wouldn't hurt to at least have the advantage of knowing what was going on with Sage before baring her soul and being the 'bigger' woman. It's like Virginia always had to be the 'bigger' woman in every situation despite the fact that she was usually much smaller, physically.

She trod over to the frosted windowpane at the side of the house. Fresh snow lay piled along the sill. Virginia stood on her toes so she could peep through the bottom corner. It was possible to see through it, though everything was blurry because of the frosted layer on the outside.

As assumed, Sage was sitting in her chair, but there was something on her face, like a handkerchief?

Virginia took off her mitten, and wiped a corner of the window. She set her eye back to the little clearing, and now could see inside the house.

Sage was wearing a homemade gag. A mixture of blood and snot was dripping out of her nose, and it looked like one of her eyes was puffy, her had askance. It was hard to tell from this angle.

She was also tied to her chair, which unless she was also an escape artist, meant that someone else was there.

Virginia pulled away from the window.

Maybe that was Sage's thing. Maybe she's into it. Maybe there's another girl there, or who knows – a guy? Virginia barely knew her. Maybe she went both ways. A little sting of jealousy crept into her, regardless.

She went back to the window, peeping in. At the far end of the house, a tall dark figure, still wearing a jacket inside the house. It was vaguely familiar, like the phantom from last night.

Virginia shook just thinking about it: the figure walking into her room, the giant thumb covering the camera lens as it set her phone on the ground.

No, this wasn't some fetish sex thing. Sage was in trouble. And if she weren't then they would forgive Virginia for what she was about to do.

Virginia crept back around to the front of the house. She popped the latch at the back of the snowmobile, and the storage compartment opened. She took off her other mitten, reached inside, and pulled out the handgun. It was so cold it felt like the metal was stuck to her hand.

She clicked the safety off, then quietly closed the storage compartment lid so the wind wouldn't slam it shut. Step by step, she snuck up the stairs, onto the front porch, her hands shaking. She was literally about to confront her demons in real life.

She slowly tested the door handle. It was open.

14

Rescue

Virginia twisted the handle slowly with her naked left hand, the cold biting into her skin. The latch quietly eased against its final resting spot at the edge of the lock. She rested her boot against the door, pushing forward with her toe to counteract the force as it moved in. She eased forward so slowly that anyone watching the door wouldn't see it opening.

And then it was wide enough she slid her body into the house sideways. She leveled the gun, sweeping it across the room.

Sage was still tied to the chair. Her neck craned as far as it could, her eyes trained on the kitchen.

In the kitchen, the tall man in the dark jacket was bent over the stove. The flames from one burner leapt high, parting ways around a metal fire-poker lying across the stovetop.

Virginia inched forward, mindfully stepping on the wooden floor where the planks met, to avoid any creaking. She walked closer to Sage's chair.

Sage rested her exhausted neck; her head circling back forward as she slumped. When she noticed Virginia, her head shot up to look at her. This was no game; her eyes were filled with surprise, fear, and hatred. Her face was damaged; blood trickled from her nose, caught by the handkerchief above her mouth. Her eyes, and cheeks had taken a beating.

The man in the kitchen turned the stove off as Virginia reached the edge of Sage's chair. He reached for the far wooden handle of the metal poker, now glowing red at the tip, and picked it up. As he turned toward Sage, he noticed Virginia, and froze.

Virginia already had the gun pointed at him. With her free hand, she tugged at the handkerchief around Sage's face, loosening it enough to squeeze it up over her head.

The man still gripped the glowing poker, his other hand raised.

Virginia poked forward with her gun. "Who are you?"

He moved imperceptibly slowly, the glowing red from the tip of the poker dipping slightly. "If you're asking about my name, it's Derek," his voice was deep, low, and gravelly.

"What the fuck were you doing in my house last night?" Virginia tried to keep her voice from trembling. Her heart raced. At least her she was able to will her hand to keep steady.

Derek lifted the poker, and his other hand. "I'm not the bad guy here. I think you don't know the whole story."

Sage choked on her bloody spit. "Virginia," she whispered. Her voice was almost gone. "Cut me loose."

"You didn't answer my question," Virginia glanced down at Sage, and back at the desk. She saw a hunting knife. She whipped her gaze back to the kitchen.

Derek had taken a step forward, but he stopped when she caught him moving.

Virginia backed up until she bumped into the desk. "You can stay right where you are, and answer me. What were you doing in my house?" She fumbled with her free hand to pick up the hunting knife.

Derek sighed. "I'll tell you true," the words slipped slowly from his mouth. "I spent my life living in that house. I miss it. I miss my wife, and daughter."

He lowered his free hand, pointing at Sage. "The real bad guy is this sinner, here. She killed my daughter. Tore my family apart."

"You fucking idiot," Sage tried to scream the words, but her it came out as a harsh whisper. "You shot your daughter right here in this house, just before you shot my daddy."

Virginia chanced a quick glance down to where Sage's ropes bound her. She slipped the knife under the rope tying her arm behind the chair, and yanked it toward her. Thankfully, Sage kept her knives way too sharp. The taught, thin rope came apart easily.

Derek took another step forward. "You brought your own brand of demons to our good forest. You weren't welcome back then, and you sure aren't welcome now."

Virginia handed the knife to Sage, then put her free hand up, cupped under the gun. Her shoulder relaxed from the tension of holding the weighty metal at an arms length for too long.

Sage sliced through her ropes, methodically working her way through until she was free.

Derek took another step forward. He was ten paces away, less with his long legs. "I left you alone, city girl. This isn't your fight."

Sage stood up, leaning on the chair for support. "This isn't anyone's fight except yours, you monster," she whispered. "You couldn't accept your daughter for who she was, so you ended her existence. There isn't anyone to blame here except yourself."

Derek grunted, launching himself toward the women. In a split second he was an arms length away, the red-hot poker aimed at Virginia.

POP.

Virginia flinched as the gun recoiled into Sage.

Sage's hands were wrapped around Virginia's, holding the gun.

Derek fell at their feet, crying out in pain. The poker burned into the wood floor.

Sage wrangled the gun from Virginia, aiming it at Derek.

Virginia turned away.

POP. POP.

Virginia dug her fingers into Sage's arms. "Holy fuck! Holy fuck, holy fuck, holy fuck."

Sage stood fast, her muscles tensed.

"Oh my god, I can't look." Virginia squirmed. "Did you seriously just kill him?"

Sage's arms relaxed, and she sat back down in the chair. She swapped the gun for a bottle of whiskey on the desk next to her.

"Can you say something please?" Virginia put her hands on her face, and looked over at Sage.

Sage sipped whiskey from the bottle. "Hard to talk. He got my neck pretty good," she whispered. She swallowed the whiskey, and made a raspy sound as she tried to clear her throat.

Virginia paced a small line back and forth. "I just fucking shot a guy. Are you kidding me?"

Sage offered her the whiskey bottle. "You didn't kill him. I did."

Virginia stopped, and stared into Sage's eyes. "I just murdered someone. What are we going to do?"

Sage set the whiskey down. "Get my goddamn dog, that's what we're going to do." She stood up on shaky legs, looking around the house. She spotted Denzel, keeled over near the kitchen. She scooped him up in her arms, and brought him back to the chair.

"What happened to Denzel?" Virginia looked over at Sage, her eyes accidentally running across Derek's body, and the pool of blood he was lying in. She involuntarily hurled up her Nutella rice bagel onto the floor next to him. Doubled over, she retched again, this time launching only bile.

"I don't know," Sage whispered. She held Denzel in her lap. He was breathing.

Virginia wiped her mouth. She shuddered, then collected herself. "This is insane." She grabbed the whiskey bottle, pouring some into her mouth. She swished it around, then spit it out on the ground.

She shook her head, her cheeks burning. "Whoa. Strong." She reached her hand out and laid it on Denzel's ribs, slowly moving in and out. "Is he going to be okay? What happened?"

Sage looked at Virginia, sadness glossing her eyes. "That monster stood outside, and waited. Caught me off guard. Denzel wouldn't let up, so I opened my front door, and the next thing I know, I'm seeing stars."

Virginia leaned in so she could hear the whispering better.

"He had this planned." Sage shook her head. "All I remember is Denzel yapping away, defending me. And this guy must have fed him something, maybe poison. Maybe just a sedative."

She stroked Denzel. "You're going to pull through, you sweet thing." Her hand came to rest on Virginia's, and they interlaced their fingers, Denzel's breath gently pushing in, and out.

Sage locked eyes with Virginia. "Thank you. This would have gone down very different if it weren't for you."

Virginia thought about the body lying behind her, the thick blood oozing into the cracks of the wood floor. She felt sick again, but there was nothing more to throw up.

"I don't know why I was such a bitch to you," Sage whispered. "I think I was just sabotaging myself. You're perfect in every way. You're young, and kind. I felt like I had nothing to offer you but my fucked up past, and here you are, involved in it."

"Sage," Virginia paused, searching for something. She gripped her hand tighter. "We actually killed someone."

Sage nodded. "Someone bad."

Virginia shook her head. "But why did you have to kill him?"

Sage stared blankly. "He deserved to die. And if I didn't kill him, he sure as hell was going to kill us."

Virginia contemplated. Her mind was spinning.

"You of all people should be able to have some understanding here," Sage took a sip of whiskey. "Everyone up here heard about your accident. Seems like the cloud of dust is following you around."

Virginia glowered. "I have fucked up plenty in my life, but that was an accident. If it wasn't I would be in jail. But this?" She unhooked her fingers from Sage's. "We murdered someone. We will go to jail. What are we supposed to do now?"

"Hey, it's going to be okay," Sage leaned forward and brought Virginia into a hug, Denzel between them. "I wasn't criticizing you for having a long string of bad luck. I get it. That dead asshole over there ruined my life because I was in love, and then came back to kill me for it."

Virginia couldn't hold it in anymore. The weight of their situation hit her: Sage's battered face, Denzel fighting for his life, the dead body on the floor behind her that she couldn't bear to look at.

Sage gripped the back of Virginia's hair, bringing their foreheads together. "I know you're scared right now, but nobody's looking for this guy, he's got no family. Plus we're in the middle of the woods. You're my closest neighbor. We're totally safe here."

A knock on the door, loud and clear.

Virginia looked at Sage's puzzled face with wild eyes.

15

No Cure

Sage reached for the gun on the desk next to her.

"Wait," Virginia hissed. "Let me answer it."

"Why?" mouthed Sage.

"Otherwise they're just going to go around and look through the window," Virginia gestured with her hand, as she backed toward the door. "And see this." She motioned in the general direction of the dead body, managing not to look at it.

Another knock at the door.

Virginia opened it a crack, pushing her foot against her end of the door so it wouldn't open any more.

Outside, Ernie peered in, seeing Virginia's body blocking the entrance.

"Oh my god, Ernie!" Virginia smiled. "I totally forgot I called you."

Ernie stumbled to find the words. A layer of snow covered his wool beanie, and shoulders, like bad dandruff. He opened his mouth to say something.

"You were right," Virginia cut him off before he could start. "I came to say goodbye to my dog, Denzel, and I realized I do like it here for now. I was missing home so bad. But you were right. I thought about it, and I'm staying."

Ernie nodded. "Okay. So you? You're okay? Everything's okay?"

Virginia nodded emphatically. "I'm great. I really appreciate you coming out in this weather. I'll have Callie get you a bonus, okay?"

"Happy to be of service, beautiful," Ernie smiled, and saluted. "You let me know if you need anything else."

Virginia nodded. "I will. Again, thank you so much!" She closed the door gently, and locked the latch. Then she tromped over to the window by Sage in her boots. Did he suspect anything? He didn't seem like it. But why would Virginia still be wearing her boots indoors?

Fortunately he didn't come to the window to inspect, even if her behavior was a little off.

Sage took another sip of whiskey, her eyes closed. "You were leaving?"

Virginia shot her a look, but realized Sage couldn't see it. "Yeah. I was, actually. I came to warn you first."

"About what?" Sage tilted her head back, wincing.

"I caught this guy in my house last night, and videotaped it." Virginia walked around the house, skirting the perimeter to get to the kitchen, so she didn't have to see the mess in the center of the floor. "I thought you might want to know there was a real life creep breaking into houses."

In the kitchen, Virginia poked through the freezer. She grabbed an unlabeled pack of frozen meat, and retraced her steps back to Sage, switching hands as the cold stung her.

"I owe you," Sage said to the ceiling.

Virginia put her hand on Sage's shoulder, handing her the plastic vacuum-sealed frozen meat. "For your face."

Sage opened her eyes, welling up at the corners, and cast a tender gaze at Virginia. "I don't blame you for leaving."

She accepted the frozen meat, and braced herself as she rested it over her swollen cheeks. "I underestimated you, and that's one of my pet peeves. People do it all the time with me. There's no apology I can make other than letting you know I'm there for you. Anything you need from me, just ask."

Virginia nodded, even though Sage couldn't see it. "Yeah, okay. I'm really freaking out about this right now."

Sage lifted her hand in front of her.

Virginia knelt down, and twined her hand into Sage's, letting the pair rest on Sage's knee.

Sage took a deep breath, sighing. "It's a mess. I'm sorry you got involved. Thank you for not letting him kill me, and whatever else he was planning. I want you to know I'll clean everything up."

"That's like the least of my concerns right now," Virginia wiped her forehead on her bicep. She realized she was flushed because she still had all her winter gear on – boots, jacket, snow pants.

"No," Sage motioned to the unspeakable thing close by. "I mean I'll clean it all up. Not just the mess, obviously."

Virginia narrowed her eyes. "I don't follow."

Sage waved her free hand. "I'll get rid of the body. This never happened. Nobody will ever find out."

"I think that legally we are in the right." Virginia squirmed. "I have video footage of this guy breaking into my house. We only shot him in self-defense. Why don't we just call the cops?"

Sage ripped the ice pack off her face, and leveled Virginia with a red-eyed glare. "Are you serious? It's a small town. They all go to the same church. The church that thinks it's a fucking crime for girls to kiss. You and I would both hang for this. Not literally, but who knows what they'd throw at us?"

Virginia could feel Sage's grip getting tighter. "Us? I just showed up."

"And pointed a gun at the deceased," Sage reminded her. "You happened to be holding that gun that I fired, and killed him with."

She pulled Virginia closer. "Look, I'm not blaming you, I'm thanking you. But facts are facts. This looks bad for both of us. This psychopath was coming after us, but he's the same guy that killed my lover, and my daddy. It looks pretty bad from that perspective."

Virginia shook her head. "I feel horrible. I can't believe this happened."

"Look at me, Virginia," Sage commanded.

Virginia lifted her eyes, and looked at Sage.

"This isn't on you," Sage's voice was cracking. "This man brought it on himself. Just like you said, he broke into your house. Why? I have no idea, but most people don't go doing things like that. He told me he was here to show me what normal people do, which seemed like a thinly veiled rape threat. I assume he was going to end my life after making me very uncomfortable."

Virginia dropped her eyes. It all made sense, in a horrible way. Sage was right, but still her stomach churned. She felt like the worst person in the world. This was far worse than the accident. That had actually been an accident. And a car. It was over so fast; Virginia didn't even have time to see what happened.

She closed her eyes, but the image of the man who was still next to her, drenched in his own blood, remained.

"Can I take a shower?" she managed.

Sage let go of her hand. "Of course. Help yourself to anything in the house. I'm sorry if I wasn't such a good hostess the last time you were here. I had a lot on my mind."

Sage lifted Denzel, and took him over to the spiral staircase. He was still breathing, but he didn't react.

Just one more thing to add to the long list of shitty things. Virginia skirted the room again, making her way into the bathroom. She took off her shoes, her coat, her snow pants, everything.

Looking at her naked body in the mirror, she felt gross. She was a serial killer now. How fragile was this thing called life? A few nights back, she could have died alone out in the woods, but Sage had come and rescued her. That whole situation was caused by the disturbed individual breaking into her house; the same human who was now lying on the floor outside the bathroom, who was alive and breathing until not that long ago.

Logically, it didn't make any sense. The guy deserved death. It seemed like he craved it. There was no reason to be broken up about that. But actually shooting someone was a whole different beast.

She looked her body over again. What good was being beautiful in such an ugly world? What was the use of acting like someone in front of a camera, when nobody knows how to act in real life? It's like a world of selfish people competing to see who can hurt each other worse.

Virginia ran the shower, waiting for it to warm. She flicked the heat lamp on. Her lips pulled at the corners into a smile.

Don't worry you're not going crazy Virginia. But this is truly funny.

Here she was, intentionally in the middle of nowhere by herself so she could hit the pause button on the drama that was her life. More accurately, here she was right now at another random hook ups' house, figuring out what to do about the dead body in the middle of the floor.

There was no cure for the kind of life she led, substances or no. There's no rehab for being the center of a continuous shit storm. She might as well just accept it, and move on.

The water was hot. Virginia got in, and let it wash over her. Like a phoenix from the ashes, maybe it could wash away her sins. Not being gay, but more like killing people, taking nice people for granted, taking herself for granted, and not truly being present for most of her life.

Virginia rested her palms on the dark blue shower tiles, letting the water take it all away, wash it down the drain. It was time for so much more than affirmations. It was time to take action, to act out her real life like she was the star she was born to be. It was time to stop talking about things, and start doing them.

A knock on the bathroom door. "Do you mind if I come in?"

Virginia turned toward it. "Yeah, of course. It's your house."

Sage opened the door, and entered. "This is becoming a pattern. Mind if I join you in there?"

"Please."

Sage undressed. She slid the glass door, and came in from behind.

Aside from her face, her body was untouched. Voluptuous in all the good ways, her curves drew the eye to all the essential areas, each one complimenting the next.

Virginia stepped in, their naked bodies touching. Her stiff nipples brushed the top of Sage's ribs as she turned a half circle around so the two women switched spots.

Sage looked Virginia up and down, backing into the stream of hot water. "I just needed…" the water covered her head, spilling down her face. She emerged from a sheet of water, finding its way around her pale contour. "I just needed you."

16

Hot

Sage leaned in, finding Virginia's lips, locking them in her own. Her hands rested easily on Virginia's sleek hips, like they'd found a new home. Hot water sprayed down her neck, pooled momentarily at her sharp collarbones, then cascaded down her breasts and on to Virginia.

Virginia closed her eyes and rose up on the balls of her feet to meet Sage's kiss. Her arms slid easily around Sage's back. She banished the thought of how mad she was at this woman only a few hours ago. It was like the electric spark of their skin touching melted any barriers she was subconsciously creating. It stoked a fire she had been trying to suppress, a deep yearning for human contact.

Virginia pushed her pelvis forward, gripping Sage's ripe ass, pulling her into grinding range. She thrust her pelvis forward, her laser-smooth womanhood rubbing against Sage's inner thigh.

Sage gasped. For being the older one, she was less experienced. She wasn't inhibited but she also wasn't aggressive. She opened her eyes to take in Virginia's beauty. It was more than just skin deep; she was kind, caring, and fucking sexy. Her eyes were inviting, her features perfectly symmetrical, her desire such a turn on.

Sage closed her eyes again, and offered her lips in worship of this being. They met Virginia's again, and again, the two of them dancing half steps until Virginia's back was pressed against the shower tiles.

Sage knelt down, catching herself on the side of the tub with her hands. Her mouth found Virginia in the center, kissing the front, and sides. Her tongue explored slowly, coasting along the edges, now diving into the wet opening.

"Oh," Virginia said, almost matter of fact. "That's good." She looked down at Sage's ultra blonde hair, wet and clinging to her scalp. She tenderly ran her fingers from the front of Sage's face to the back of her neck, aligning her hair behind her ears.

Sage found an even rhythm, licking from the back to the front. Her calculated movements dipped her chin over, and over, and over again. Her cheeks pressed into Virginia's inner thighs, her tongue widening every time she reached Virginia's firm clit.

Virginia couldn't stop sliding her back down the tiles. Her knees were giving out, the pleasure so intense she couldn't stand. Her arms scrambled for anything to grab onto, but the only thing in reach was Sage's head. She put out one arm and stroked the back of Sage's hair.

Sage backed up to maintain her position, hot water now splashing on her back, her neck, the crown of her head. It flowed over her face and down into her mouth. She licked her lips, and continued on all fours, not missing a beat.

Virginia shifted her feet, and lay flat. She gripped the sides of the tub, pulling her pelvis up into Sage's mouth. Her eyes squeezed shut, her mouth open, her breaths coming in hard and fast.

Sage tilted her head just slightly, keeping the tempo but changing the location. She increased the pressure, and Virginia cried out.

"Oh my god that's so good!" Virginia screamed. "Please, please, please..." but she didn't finish her thought, her body shaking violently as her butt cheeks squeezed together. Her head pressed hard against the back of the bathtub, her fingers balled into fists, with nothing to grab onto.

"Oh, wow," Virginia propped herself up, wiping stray water off her face. "You spoil me."

Sage grinned, and leaned in to plant a sloppy kiss on Virginia's mouth.

Virginia could taste herself. She shivered despite the heat lamp, and the warm water, her muscles releasing tension. She could feel a slow burn in her back hamstrings where she was holding herself up.

"My turn," Virginia flashed a devilish grin, righting her body to make space on the bottom of the bathtub.

Sage swept her hair over one side of her shoulder, her pear shaped bottom placed firmly on her feet.

Virginia leaned in and kissed her mouth, her palms walking her body over Sage, pushing her back.

Sage leaned her head back, making room for Virginia to kiss her cheeks, her neck, her shoulders.

Virginia paused when the got to Sage's pink nipples, licking them from bottom to top. Her mouth enveloped them, her teeth grazing the soft edges until they popped to attention.

She brought her hand up Sage's leg, her fingers catching the warm water flowing over. When she got to the middle, she circled her first two fingers a few times before dipping them in.

Sage caught a breath, her hand dipping down to touch herself.

Virginia shook her head, smiling. "Uh, uh." She leaned down and moved Sage's hand away with her face.

Sage rested her hand on her inner thigh, pulling her skin tighter.

Virginia explored with her fingers, rotating her wrist so they twisted into the walls. She brought her face down to the platinum bush, her chin brushing the water droplets clinging to the golden curls.

She deftly darted her tongue around, inside. She quickly flicked it back, and forth over the bump in the center, feeling it swell with a rush of heat as she flicked it up, and down. The warm water from the shower soaked her hair, running in rivulets down her flawless features.

"Mmmph," Sage reached out for Virginia's face, as tremors shook her. "That…"

Virginia stuck her tongue all the way in and French kissed Sage's soft, femininity.

"That's…" Sage tried again, but she was melting. Her words fused into guttural moaning.

Virginia started pumping again with her fingers, following up with soft tongue-lashing at any exposed area.

"It's so good," Sage cried. Her body was gelatin, letting Virginia work her magic.

Virginia dipped the thumb of her other hand into her juicy self. Then she stuck her hand under Sage's butt, and squeezed her thumb up, parting the crack, and into the hole.

Sage's eyes opened wide as she gasped. "Whoa! What are you doing?"

Virginia kept licking her. "Do you like it?" She wiggled her thumb, keeping rhythmic pressure as she pushed her fingers in with her other hand.

"Uhhn." Sage moaned, and lifted her head to look down. "I just... it's new."

Virginia chuckled softly, increasing the pressure of her fingers, her thumb, her tongue. She switched to broad strokes, covering more area, and pushing hard against Sage's swollen mound.

"I do," gasped Sage. "I do like it, I do, I do!" She tried to pull away as she climaxed, but Virginia held her firmly in place.

"Uhnnn, uhnn, UHNNN!" Sage squealed with delight, her toes curling. She opened her eyes again, her unrestrained smile beaming up at Virginia.

Virginia slowly worked her way out of Sage.

"Oh my goodness," Sage stood up into the shower stream, which had turned from hot, to warm. "Just in time."

Sage and Virginia hurriedly soaped up one last time in the remnants of acceptably warm water, cooling rapidly.

Sage turned the water off. "I have a confession."

Virginia raised her eyebrows.

"I've touched myself every night while thinking about you, since the day I met you." Sage's pale cheeks flushed a hot pink.

Virginia smiled. "And here I thought I was going to leave today, and never get a chance to do that to you."

Sage moved her face closer to Virginia's. "You're my hero, today."

They toweled off, enjoying the heat lamp.

Virginia looked at the door, and sighed. She let the air out slowly.

Sage met her eyes. "I cleaned up while you were in here."

Virginia looked back, a blank expression on her face.

"It's not perfect," Sage added. "I wasn't expecting," she searched for the right words, but there were none. "Do you want to stay here?" She reached her hand out for Virginia's.

Virginia squeezed Sage's hand.

They stood there in silence, the orange glow of the light above casting warm tones on their skin.

"Could you go first?" Virginia asked.

Sage opened the door, and led the way wearing only her towel. She ushered Virginia into the main room, and toward the spiral staircase.

Virginia averted her gaze, just in case. But the room felt lighter, more at ease – even more so than when she had first come here in her panic.

"I don't know what to do now," Sage said, stepping up the spiral stairs. "I'm exhausted but it's not even dinnertime." She reached the landing, and crawled across the bed.

Denzel lay in a cocoon of blankets. Aside from his deep breathing, he made no movement to react to Sage's sudden appearance.

Virginia rested her hand on Sage's shoulder, hovering close behind her.

"He seems fine," Sage wrapped Denzel up in the top blanket that had slipped off him.

They watched him breathe, raising and lowering his blankets. It wasn't much, but it was reassuring nonetheless.

"Do you have any good books?" Virginia nodded toward a tiny bookshelf at the far edge of the attic.

Sage turned to face her. "I'm a little ashamed that most of my library is composed of eBooks," she waved her hand around the attic, "for an obvious lack of space. I do still have a few physical books I could never let go of."

Virginia looked through the volumes. "Anything you've written?"

Sage lay down, and pointed at a few of the books. "They're in here, most of them. Although, I've been told my writing is too sparse, and action packed."

"Sounds like every script I've ever read," Virginia looked over at Sage, reading her. "Are we supposed to process what just happened?"

"The sex?" Sage smiled.

Virginia bit Sage's shoulder, gently. "Like, what are you supposed to do after some fucked up shit like that goes down? Is there something we're supposed to be doing right now?"

Sage shrugged. "It's my first time, thankfully. I feel like I got my ass kicked. I feel sick to my stomach. But I don't feel guilty for any of it."

"Yeah, me neither." Virginia crawled back to the bed, and covered herself up in blankets. "I was wondering if I was just heartless."

Sage's towel dropped to the ground as she crawled under the covers next to Virginia, a book in her hand. She rested her other hand over Virginia's chest. "You're one of those rare people that still has a heart. But the world has thrown plenty of stuff your way to test it."

They both opened their books, eyes struggling to read in the dim lighting. In moments, they were fast asleep.

17

Snow Day

Virginia woke to something warm, and wet licking her face. Something meaty. She opened her eyes to see Denzel's face hovering over her, tongue ready for action.

"Denzel!" she withdrew her arms from the covers and flung them around his neck, burying her face in his furry body as she kissed him.

Denzel licked her anywhere he could reach, coating her neck, and shoulders with slobbery love.

In a heartbeat, Sage was propped up, blinking the sleep from her eyes. She wrapped her arms around Virginia, and Denzel, squeezing them tight. "Good morning," she muffled into Virginia's back. "It's good to be alive."

Denzel switched to licking Sage, working his way past her hair, and into her cheeks.

"I can't tell you how happy I am to see you," Sage's voice was returning. "Both of you." She rolled out from under the covers, and made her way to the stairs. "Pee break."

Virginia held Denzel close, rubbing his shoulders, and back. "You changed my life when you showed up at my doorstep. Thank you," she whispered. She shut her eyes as Denzel licked the lids. "Alright, alright. Too much!" She pushed Denzel away for a moment.

"No, it's never too much." She sat up, and lifted her chin as she pulled Denzel in again.

She glanced down at Sage's book. The cover was sparse, but beautiful. Layers of pink gradually getting darker from the top down, the title in bold declared Adventure Heart.' In big, bold font at the bottom was 'Sage Volland.'

She picked it up and marveled at the fact that Sage made this thing – this piece of art. In a weird way it was like when other girls in the past were in awe of the fact that Virginia was the person who made these movies that they could go see in theaters. It was nice to be on the flip side of it, to get some perspective.

Denzel put his paw on the book, pushing it down to the ground.

"You're right, I'm not being present." Virginia set the book by the side of the bed, and hoisted herself to her feet, as much as the triangular attic space allowed. She walked naked down the spiral stairs with Denzel a step behind her. She braced for the grotesque image of a man slumped out on the floor, but the area was empty. As she got closer she saw it was as clean as it had been before the incident, save for a scorched black mark in the wood where the hot poker fell.

Sage stood naked by the stove, stirring something in a pan. The savory smell of garlic, and onion permeated the air, saturating the senses.

Virginia's mouth salivated like she could already taste it. It had been a rough few days of skipping meals, but nothing she wasn't already accustomed to with her tumultuous production lifestyle back home. The sight of a woman cooking naked touched on something primal, bringing up warm, fuzzy feelings that somehow everything was going to be okay.

It was funny to discover that everything she thought she would escape on this rehab vacation came around full circle. It didn't matter where she was in the world, the fact remained that it was still Virginia that was there. She might as well embrace who she was.

A pee break was definitely in order.

"That smells really good," she passed by the stove.

Sage looked up and smiled genuinely at her.

Virginia stepped into the bathroom, and sat down on the toilet. There was something very strange about today, if only because nothing seemed strange. She and Sage seemed like a happy couple, and the menacing phantom from yesterday was out of sight, and soon might even be out of mind.

Months of trying to be still, trying to calm her mind, trying to escape her path of destruction amounted to this.

Maybe Virginia wasn't addicted to substances after all. Maybe it was just those visceral, extraordinary experiences that she needed in her life. And was there anything wrong with not wanting to be bored?

Denzel scratched at the door.

She laughed quietly to herself. She'd spend the winter pondering deep and metaphysical things, only to face the true reality of her nature – cuddling between a dog, and a beautiful woman.

Virginia flushed, and washed her hands. She decided to do a little touch up downstairs, because who knows what breakfast would lead to? She dried up, and opened the bathroom door.

Denzel hopped up on his hind two legs, thrusting his front paws up at her.

"You sure have a lot of energy," Virginia noted, grabbing him in her arms. "You must be really well rested."

Denzel licked her décolletage, then smashed his forehead into her collarbone.

Virginia walked toward the kitchen. "Do you want me to put something on for breakfast?"

Sage grinned. "You could put plates on the counter." She puckered up.

Virginia closed the distance, and dropped some long, slow kisses on her lips. She fluttered her eyelashes, and composed herself. She set Denzel on a cushioned chair, and squeezed back into the kitchen.

The kitchen was intuitive, partly because it was ridiculously small. There was only room enough for her body next to the sink, and she was still brushing shoulders with Sage at the stove. Opening the cabinets required dodging them as they came toward her face.

Virginia found two plates, and set them on the mini counter next to the stove. "Should I ask?" She motioned toward the empty space in the center of the room, and the black burn mark on the floor.

"Sure," Sage replied. "If you want to know."

"I do," Virginia plucked two forks from a drawer. "And I don't."

Sage shoveled a veggie egg scramble onto each of their plates. She slapped a slab of meat down on one of them.

"Can I try a bite?" Virginia poked the meat with one of the forks.

Sage cast her an enquiring glance. "I thought you didn't eat red meat." She cut a chunk off the end of the slab, and flipped it to the other plate.

Virginia snatched two napkins from a wrought iron holder, and wrapped them around the forks. "Usually I don't, but I really respect that you went to the effort to catch it yourself." She picked up her plate, and walked to the chairs in the living room.

Denzel abandoned his cushions, and came panting to see if anything accidentally, or intentionally dropped.

The two famished women ate in silence, more because they were ravenous than for any lack of warmth between them.

Sage slipped Denzel a prized piece of meat, and some eggs from the scramble.

Virginia watched the two of them, considering her own diet. Dogs ate pretty much only meat, so why wasn't her body able to? Was it the chemicals that people always ranted about? Or the vibrations of the beasts before they were slaughtered?

She stuck her fork in, piercing the greyish hunk of red meat on her plate. Pink juice came out. She brought the non-fish meat to her lips for the first time in almost ten years. It smelled wonderful: savory, succulent, pan-fried, garlic salty tang. And it tasted alive, bursting with flavor. Her taste buds popped, singing praises to this delicacy.

"Pretty good, huh?" Sage was watching.

146

Virginia nodded, chewing for what seemed like an eternity. Each bite down offered diminishing rewards, the flavor quickly washed away. Soon the meat was just a thick, chewy piece of flavorless gristly muscle tissue. She swallowed it anyways, it wasn't bad, just blah.

Sage picked up a steamy mug and clinked it to another one resting on the desk. She blew on it, then slowly sipped it.

Virginia noticed a guitar case, under a checkered, tablecloth-sized piece of fabric. She pointed her toe toward it. "You play?"

Sage nodded. "You?"

"No, but I love singing." Virginia set her empty plate on the desk. She went to the case, taking the fabric off it. She laid it out flat, unbuckling the metal clasps that kept it firmly shut. "What's your jam?"

"Slow stuff," Sage set her mug down, and dabbed at her mouth with a napkin. She wiped her fingers on it, tip by tip. "I love gospel, soulful, blues."

"Like Jonie Brynne?" Virginia gently scooped the guitar from the soft felt inside of the case. She handed it to Sage.

Denzel hopped down, and poked his nose into the empty case for a better sniff of it.

Sage instinctually tuned the strings, matching them until it was in pitch. "Are you kidding me? I grew up on Jonie. Always loved her, always will."

Virginia sat at the edge of her chair, across from Sage.

"Forgive me, Jonie." She strummed a few chords, her picking hand expertly soloing out a few notes as she blurred from riff to riff. "I'm a little rusty."

Both women softened, memories flooding back as the song progressed.

Sage paused, looking at Virginia before she started the first chorus.

Virginia nodded. They started in together:

"When the sun shines down, and the leaves fall away

I see you there behind me, fading from the grey

You watch me now, you hold me still

I always did, I always will

Love you, love you, love you.

Sage bopped her head, softly tapping her bare foot in time with the tempo, consumed by the music.

Virginia closed her eyes, letting it carry her away. She sang a high harmony to accompany Sage's lower register.

Denzel chimed in with a high-pitched howl whenever a long note presented the opportunity.

As they held the last note, Sage let the guitar strings reverberate. "Not bad for our first time together."

Virginia rubbed the back of her neck, settling the hairs standing on end. "I was in a band as a kid, and I think we never came close to anything like that."

Sage stood up, and set the guitar back in the case. She lightly brushed Virginia with her hand as she passed. "I won't kick you out like last time… but I do have some unsavory plans today."

Virginia swallowed, a lump suddenly forming in her throat. She picked up on things quick.

"You're welcome to stay," Sage offered. "It might give you some memories you'd rather not have. You can't unsee a thing, you know."

"Of course," Virginia stood up and wrapped her arms around Sage, showering her with kisses. "Are you going to be okay here alone?"

Sage sighed. "I thought so for many, many years." She kissed Virginia back. Then she adjusted her head to a more conversational distance. "May I come by your place later?"

Denzel hopped up to join Virginia, by licking Sage in her vulnerable neck region.

Virginia beamed. "I'd be delighted." She pecked Sage on the cheek, then ruffled Denzel's fur.

"Hey," Sage picked up a piece of soft fabric, and tossed it to Virginia.

Virginia leaned in and caught it. She unrolled a soft, black ski mask. She slipped it over her head, and gave Sage a thumbs up.

In the entryway, Virginia bundled up in her very unwelcome thick winter wear. Though it was way too hot for the plush heat of Sage's cabin, she could see little flurries of snow blowing by outside. The nonstop storm they had been enduring was relentless, though mild at the moment.

Outside, there was a beauty to the fresh, soft flakes, layering powder on top of the icy thicker snow on the ground. Inuit peoples had like a hundred words for snow, but they probably also had a lot more time on their hands. Somewhere deep inside, a fountain of fresh source energy bubbled up inside of Virginia. The trek home seemed warm, and she couldn't stop smiling as she appreciated the beauty of this winter wonderland.

When she came to the snowy edge demarcating her yard, she saw fresh snowmobile tracks, and two sets of footprints leading up to the house. Living out here was making her a verified tracker.

Fucking now what?

It was more annoyance than fear, as Virginia steered her boots into the prints already on the ground, making her way up the path to her front door. There was just so much going on already, how was it possible to heap more bullshit on the pile?

She didn't have a gun, or a bat, or anything that could even be construed as a weapon. But at this point, it didn't matter. She had her temper, and that would be enough to deal with whoever was in her house.

She opened the front door hard, banging it into the coat closet.

Inside, a woman screamed.

Virginia stepped to the edge of the entryway to see around the fireplace. She lifted up her ski mask.

In the living room, Callie opened her arms. "Virginia! Oh my god, you scared me!"

18

The Big One

Callie held Virginia close. "Girl, you look happy!" She danced in place.

"And you look tired." Virginia grinned, holding on to Callie's shoulders.

Callie bobbled her head back and forth. "I flew up when Ernie called," she sniffled, wiping her nose. "Took an overnight, because I had to see for myself."

"Can I get you something to drink?" Virginia sidestepped Callie into the kitchen.

"Oh my god, yes please," Callie followed her into the kitchen. "I am literally dying for something warm, like hot chocolate?"

Virginia reached up to a cabinet, and pulled out a tin of Williams Sonoma hot cocoa, and a box of fancy square marshmallows. She took out two Christmas themed mugs with tasteful holly, and candy prints on the outside.

"Of course you have this set up all nice," Callie rubbed her hands together. "You have the best taste in everything. I take it you enjoyed your winter staycation?"

"There were moments," Virginia grinned, and set up some almond milk on the stove to boil. "You had to see what?" She narrowed her eyes.

"I want you to know this is coming from a place of love," Callie put her hand on Virginia's heart.

Virginia put her hand over Callie's. "Always."

"Good," Callie patted the hand on Virginia's heart. "When Ernie called me I knew it was one of two things. And because I believe in you – always have, always will – I hoped it was that you wanted to come back because you finally kicked it."

They both took a deep breath.

"And here you are," Callie added. "Safe, sober, and happy. Seriously girl, you're radiant. I know you met someone up here."

Virginia grinned. "I did. You know me well." She turned to the stove, and poured off the steamy almond milk into the cocoa cups. "But I had this huge revelation today." She stirred the cocoa, and tossed a couple marshmallows into each cup. "The drugs weren't the problem."

Callie looked back at Virginia, stone faced.

Virginia explained with her hands. "The drugs made the problem worse. In all fairness, I had a lot of fun. But I also did some things I'm not proud of. I know Richard is still finding space in his heart to forgive me."

Callie fixed a knowing look on Virginia, and turned up the corner of her mouth.

"And rightfully so," Virginia added. "Tell him I said I'm sorry yet again, and this time when I was sober, if you think that will help." She sighed. "Being high all the time, and getting wasted wasn't to prove a point, or because I had some dark secrets. I know there are lots of people who need a fix to get out of their heads. But that wasn't my thing."

"Okay," Callie said, tracking.

"Honestly, I was bored," Virginia handed a mug to Callie, and clinked her mug against it. "I know that sounds like a simple explanation, but after all this time to sit and think about it, I just need some adventure. I don't need the drama necessarily, but I need something exhilarating."

Callie nodded rhythmically. "Yes. I agree. I think you're onto something. So now, what can we do to get you into some adventures where you don't wreck your car at the end of the night?"

"I can always blow my money on fancy vacations," Virginia looked around the quaint kitchen. She set her mug of cocoa down, and grabbed Callie gently by the shoulders, shaking her back and forth. "Challenge me girl, get me into a nice juicy role. Something where I'm not just eye candy that makes out with a dude at the end of the movie."

Callie laughed, trying unsuccessfully to keep the cocoa in her cup. "Oh, girl. It's moments like this that I live for. And not just because I love your company."

"What?" Callie brought her face close to Callie's. "What is it? You have news."

Callie smiled, setting her mug of cocoa on the counter. "I do. Are you ready for this?"

Virginia hopped up and down, still clutching Virginia's sweater. "Yes! Yes!"

"Okay," Callie looked down to collect herself, then looked Virginia straight in the eyes. "When I got the offer, I told them that your answer was conditional on a few things. Number one, you were first billed... with Ryan Duckworth."

"Are you kidding me?" Virginia let go of Callie, and hopped around the room. "I love Ryan! He's the sweetest, most professional... how did you do that?"

Callie put her hand up. "There's more."

"Residuals?"

Callie flapped her lips. "Please, would I ever not get you sweet residuals?"

Virginia swooped in. "Okay, then what?"

"Second," Callie put up two fingers, "it's already slated for a November release.

Virginia stared at Callie, her jaw lowering slowly.

"Yes, yes, yes! Right?" Callie waved her hands in the air. "This could be the defining moment where you become a household name." She put her hand behind Virginia's neck, bringing her face in close. "I told you before you checked into this cabin, girl. I'm in it for the long haul. I know you're so much more than a couple of front-page stories. You're the real deal."

Virginia's eyes stung. She couldn't stop her lip from trembling.

Callie let her arm drop, giving Virginia some space to wipe the tears forming at the corners of her eyes. "Third," Callie picked up her mug of cocoa again, blowing steam off the top. "They gave you three days to take the offer."

"Oh," Virginia set her hands on her hips. "That's a good thing?"

Callie thrust a finger into the air, wiggling it. "I got you two weeks. But it started a couple of days ago."

Virginia cocked her head.

"I wanted to tell you in person." Callie sipped her cocoa. "And this isn't a once in a lifetime opportunity. If it's too much pressure, you can say no."

Virginia circled behind Callie, hugging her from behind, her arms dodging the cocoa mug. "I love you. You're the best. Although that was a really strange way of ordering the importance of each detail."

Callie laughed. "Yeah, I didn't really plan a big speech. I got all excited for you." She took another sip of cocoa. "Also, you seriously do have the best taste. This is delicious."

Virginia let go of Callie, and picked up her own mug, sipping it. "It is." She opened the fridge. "I know tuna salad doesn't technically go with chocolate, but I've been making this killer Mediterranean style spicy spread with rice crackers."

"Yes, please! I'm starving." Callie looked in the fridge. "Good, I see that Ernie's been doing well."

"Yup," Virginia pulled out a glass Tupperware of tuna salad, and some crackers from the cabinet. "He's a character alright, but super reliable. Sweet, too." She pulled out two plates, and dolloped the tuna salad in the center, adorning the side with crackers, snippets of washed grapes, and raspberries.

"Come enjoy the house," Virginia handed a plate to Callie, then took hers into the living room. "And you can take your boots off inside the house."

"Oh yeah," Callie kicked off a pair of Uggs at the entryway. "I wasn't sure what the etiquette was around here." She settled herself into a chair in the living room. "Did you know that Ernie drove me here in one of those... landspeeder things that goes on snow?"

Virginia laughed. "Snowmobile. You get used to them. Actually, I kind of like how they vibrate, and rock you up, and up, and up," she demonstrated with her hand.

"Oh my goodness," Callie grinned. "You're unstoppable. Speaking of which, tell me about the new girl. I want details."

Virginia cocked her head to the side. "The new girl, is a woman."

"Ooh, someone mature. Maybe refined?" Callie took a bite of tuna cracker.

"In some ways, yeah," Virginia set down her plate, fishing in her bag for Sage's book. She set it on the table in front of Callie. "She's a bit of a backwoods hunter, and whiskey drinker. She's also an author."

Callie stopped chewing, glancing from the book to Virginia. "Seriously? Sage Volland? Are you seriously kidding me right now?"

Virginia shrugged, waiting for the punch line. "She didn't know who I was, either. She's not into film."

"Yeah, I know that," Callie picked up the book, looking at the front, and back. "She has like a half dozen New York Bestsellers and she's never sold the film rights to anything."

"Yeah, that sounds like her." Virginia popped a grape in her mouth. "I don't think she really cares."

Callie shook the book, then set it back down on the table. "When you have that many fans, there are plenty of people who do care." She looked back to Virginia. "I thought she was Canadian. What's she doing here?"

A thoughtful smile crossed Virginia's face. "Same thing I am, I guess. Just going about it differently."

Callie dipped another cracker in tuna. "This is too good. I know you don't use recipes, but you have to tell me what you put in it."

Virginia closed her eyes. "Tuna, olives, red onion, feta cheese, red pepper flakes, pepperoncini. Then some olive oil, and balsamic?"

Callie chewed slowly. "So good," she said over her mouthful. She picked up another cracker, and pointed it at Virginia. "You think she wants to move to LA?"

Virginia blushed, picking her grapes off the stem. "It's just sex. And stuff."

Callie looked incredulously at Virginia.

"I like her dog," Virginia offered. "I love her dog, he's a cute little black puppy. I named him Denzel."

Callie put her hand out, tipping it back and forth. "Meh, borderline racist, but I still love the name. May I also point out that you picked out the name for your lady's dog?"

Virginia smirked. "I would say it's not what you think, but you're too smart for that. Then again, we haven't really talked about anything official."

"Good," Callie finished her tuna spread, and licked her fingers. "If she needs any more convincing to move away from this misery other than your beautiful face, I could get her a movie deal on one of her books, like tonight. Hell, I could probably get her a deal on all of her books by tonight."

Virginia sighed, letting her back relax into the sofa. It had been a long few days. She followed Callie with her eyes as she heaved herself up, and walked over to where Virginia sat.

"Girl I'm so proud of you," Callie sat down and wrapped her arms around Virginia. "I knew you could do it," she paused, thinking. "But you did it."

19

Breaking the Ice

Virginia and Callie sat giggling, their cocoa mugs empty. They both jumped at the knock on the front door, and then it opened.

"Hello?" Sage called from the entryway. She unzipped her backpack, and Denzel scuttled out, running into the living room.

"Sage!" Virginia called back.

Denzel yipped when he saw Callie. He jumped up on the couch next to her and licked her arm, and shoulder.

"Oh are you kidding me?" Callie leaned into it, and hugged Denzel. "Aren't you just precious?" She let him lick her face as she brought it in close to his.

Sage stood there watching, her boots off.

Virginia hopped up, gliding across the room. She threw her arms around Sage, showering her with kisses.

Sage accepted Virginia's embrace with one arm, her eyes on Callie.

Callie ruffled Denzel's fur, then stood politely. "Callie," she said. She extended her hand. "I'm Virginia's heterosexual, and married agent." She tossed Sage a knowing grin.

"Well, there was that one night," Virginia chuckled.

"One night doesn't change things," Callie quipped. "Every girl's a little curious."

Sage reluctantly took Callie's hand, shaking it. "I brought over my ice-fishing gear. I thought it might be good to get some outdoor air."

"Yes," Virginia squeezed Sage. "That sounds wonderfully quirky."

Callie looked between the two of them. "And romantic. V, do you mind if I crash in the guest room?"

"Take my bedroom, it's warmer," Virginia offered. "Or at least grab some blankets off my bed." She motioned to the gas fireplace. "This doesn't do much."

Callie stretched her arms, yawning. "It only makes me that much more proud of you, girl. I couldn't last two days in a frigid place like this."

"The warm parts make up for it," Virginia cracked a smile, tossing her head back to look at Sage. "We just had the most fabulous hot cocoa. Would you like some?"

"No thanks," Sage warmed up to the scenario. "I had coffee."

"In case I don't see you before I fly back home," Callie walked toward the staircase, gently putting her hand on Sage's shoulder as she passed. "I'm a huge fan. Velvet Gloves was my favorite, if I had to choose."

Sage nodded. "It was nice to meet you."

"The pleasure was all mine," Callie dipped her head as she passed them, then hopped up the stairs with a giddy twist in her heels.

Denzel ran to the staircase, and bounded up after Callie.

Virginia watched her disappear into the hallway upstairs. She leaned into Sage and whispered, "Are we really going ice fishing? Or was that code?"

Sage turned her head and found Virginia's soft lips near her face, finding a good use for them. "Come on, let's go while it's still sunny."

Virginia snuck a glance out the window. Snow was blowing lightly. "This is sunny?"

They geared up in their thickest winter wear.

Sage passed Virginia a spare pair of gloves that resembled something a shark wrangler might wear as armor. She picked up her bags, and a wooden staff she had brought over.

As they stepped outside, Virginia was thankful for the extra layers. She followed Sage around her yard, to the back of the house, and down to the lake.

"If you need a hand with your dock, or your boat, just let me know," Sage crunched through the snow ahead. "Next fall, obviously. We can't do much about it now."

Next fall? Sage knew this was a temporary thing, right?

They walked to the edge of the lake, where a stone barrier wall dropped down to the frozen shallows.

Sage set her backpack and duffle bag on the stone, hopping down onto the ice. She picked up the bags, and took a step onto the ice. She reached her hand out.

"Are you sure this is a good idea?" Virginia stood looking down at the lake's edge, both palms flattening her gloves as she pushed back against a phantom resistance, like she was afraid the wind would betray her.

"Don't you trust me?" Sage held her arm in the air. "We've been through a lot together."

Virginia reached her hand toward Sage's despite her buckling knees. "I don't know how those two things would benefit each other, but here goes." She jumped down onto the ice, slipping as her boots dug through the snow.

"Okay," Sage grabbed Virginia and righted her. Then she tapped ahead of them with her staff. "Rule number one, don't jump on the ice." She walked ahead, dragging Virginia along with her.

"Got it," Virginia leaned her butt back, offering some resistance.

"Good," Sage let go of Virginia's hand. "Rule two, spread out." She walked a few paces ahead. "That way if you fall in, I can rescue you. And if I fall in, at least it wasn't you."

Virginia stopped. "Are you sure we should be going this far out?"

Sage slowed her pace. "The whole lake is frozen over. We're safe." She kept tapping the staff in front of her. "Probably."

Virginia sighed. It was cold. It was dangerous. But at least it wasn't sitting around indoors all day. She tried to keep up.

The snow was mild enough that she could look up and see the sky. It was more pale grey than blue.

Ahead, Sage set down her backpack, and duffle bag. She pulled out a plastic box, some metal bits, and two collapsible chairs, which she set up. She beckoned.

Virginia caught up, cautiously stepping into Sage's vicinity.

Sage drilled into the ice with an auger drill, jerking, and twisting with calculated force. "Were you and Callie ever a thing?"

Virginia backed up a step. "Are you sure that's safe? Won't the ice just keep cracking, until we both fall in?"

Sage punched through the ice, then pulled the auger out of the hole. "Done." She turned to Virginia. "You don't make it long up in these woods if you don't know what you're doing."

Virginia patted her boot on the ice in front of her, taking a small, tentative step forward. "Fair enough. You are very practical." She tested the next spot, slowly closing the distance towards Sage. "So I was never romantically involved with Callie. She's been married to a really great guy, Richard, as long as I've known her. But, full disclosure, a few of my friends and I did satisfy her curiosity one time. More accurately, one weekend. We were all tripping hard on some medical grade MDMA, and I remember very little of it. I actually didn't believe the stories until my ex showed me some video footage of it."

Virginia stood by Sage now, watching her extend a collapsible fishing rod. "Honestly, when I didn't have a reason to not be completely wasted, I indulged beyond what should be the human limits. It's why I'm up here. Almost everyone around me just assumed I was going to overdose before I had the chance to burn out."

Sage handed Virginia a metal thermos. "How do you feel now?"

"Cold," Virginia forced a smile. "Vulnerable. A little bit judged? But I don't blame you for that."

Sage reached out and took Virginia's glove in her glove. "I'm older than you. It doesn't mean I'm any wiser. I've been learning a thing or two being around you. But I want you to know that I'm not judging you. I've had exes. I've created some problems trying to run from my demons. I'm still in the thick of that phase, I think."

Sage opened her thermos, and steam lingered around the opening before rising to meet the snow. "Anyways, we're here. Let's be here." She sipped whatever was inside.

Virginia opened her thermos, and sniffed it. Some kind of herbal tea. She sipped it. It was the perfect heat to warm the body on a day like this.

Sage plunked the fishing line with something on it into the water. She set the pole on a wooden contraption, and sat back in one of the chairs.

Virginia copied her and sat back in the other chair, holding her thermos. "What do we do now?"

"We just sit," Sage sat. "And wait."

Virginia sat. "What should we talk about?"

Sage sipped her thermos. "I just like to think. Listen to nature."

"Okay," Virginia looked all the way around. It was like a screensaver out here, shades of blues and light off-whites, with nothing to focus on. Tiny powdery flakes fell slowly, enhancing the scene.

Sage passed Virginia a pair of earmuffs that looked like noise-canceling headphones.

Virginia clamped them on, and realized how cold her ears were getting without them. Oh these Northern folk, and their inventions to stave off death.

An indeterminate amount of time passed. Virginia opened her eyes only to ensure that Sage was still there, and that an errant pack of wolves was not silently descending on them. The cold now stung her eyeballs. She could see that Sage was doing the same thing, though maybe not for the same reasons.

Virginia thought she imagined a tiny bell ringing, until she saw Sage hop out of her fold-up chair, and attend to the fishing pole.

Sage lifted the line by hand. A long, fat fish was stuck to the end of it. The fish wriggled this way, and that, but Sage set it on the surface of the frozen lake, an arm's length from the hole.

The fish paused for a moment, its sideways eye searching the sky.

Sage picked up a wooden club from her bundle of tools, and brought it down on the fish's head with a thick plop.

The fish gave one last shudder, and opened its fins.

Sage unhooked it, then dropped the lure back into the watery hole. She tossed the limp fish into the empty bucket with a thud. "You want to try the next one?"

Virginia stood up, stretching her legs. Joints were liable to get stuck in this weather if you didn't move them often. She sauntered over to Sage, and picked up the club. It was surprisingly heavy for how small it was. The handle was wrapped in wood. The body was polished with wax, a few dry splintery areas at the top that had seen plenty of use.

She stood over the hole, admiring the perfectly circular nature of it. Or was it a cylinder? Like a tiny portal to another realm – which must be what it feels like to a fish – happily finding your meal one moment, then yanked into the sky the next.

Sage reset the bell, and the wooden rod holding contraption.

Within minutes, the rod bowed again.

Sage watched Virginia, motionless.

Virginia's heart beat. Old school learning by doing. She pulled the line, but the fish was strong, and offered plenty of resistance. Virginia dug her heels into the snow-covered ice, and brought her club wielding arm under the line, pulling the cord around her. She leveraged her weight, and the fish popped out of the hole. It flapped onto the ice and lay there for a moment.

That was all Virginia needed to bring the club down, heavy and true. It found its mark on the side of the fish's scaly head. Virginia raised the club again, just in case, but the fish gave the telltale death spasm. She opened her mouth in thanks, relief, and pride, all rolled into one.

Sage held both mittens in the air. Then she leaned over to help unhook the lure from the fish's mouth, and toss it into the bucket.

After four fish mostly filled the bucket, they called it a day.

Sage walked back along the ice, tapping ahead with her wooden staff.

Virginia kept a healthy distance, just in case. But it felt solid now, she felt safe. She also felt lightheaded; the cold sneaking under the muffs to get to her ears was getting to be too much. The skyline merged with the perimeter of the lake, steely metallic grey.

She stopped, as she realized there were rocks jutting up through the ice. She looked up and saw Sage standing atop the rock wall, her hand extended.

Virginia hefted the bucket with both hands, passing it up to Sage.

Sage set the bucket down, and reached down once more to help Virginia up. They walked in quiet through the forest, up to Virginia's front door.

"So I usually come across as socially awkward," Sage paused. "Because I am. But if you want to have some girl time with your agent, I get it. And also I'm feeling really inspired to get back to writing – but I wanted to spend the day with you."

Virginia kissed Sage on each cheek, keeping her face close. "Thank you for telling me. I really appreciate that you can tell me what you want. I do want to hang out with Callie; she's like my best friend as much as she is my agent. If you need a break from writing and want to drop by, she's also kind of star struck with you. And I like you a lot."

Sage nodded.

"It's not weird to be talented, and need time to work on your craft," Virginia blew kisses as she backed up to the front stoop. "I really get that."

Sage looked down at the bucket of trout. "Why don't you both come up for dinner tonight? Unless you want me to leave you some of these to clean."

"I would love that," Virginia flashed a smile that melted the snowflakes blowing around her. "We'll see you later!"

Sage waved, and hiked up the mountain toward her hill.

Virginia opened her door, and walked inside.

A black streak rushed toward her, yipping, and jumping up into her thighs.

"Denzel!" Virginia braced for impact, grabbing the beast as he rammed her. "Did mama Sage forget you?" She glanced over her shoulder. "Or did she leave you here so she could get some peace and quiet?"

Denzel licked Virginia's face as she bent down, pulling her boots off.

20

Home

Virginia held Denzel to her chest, walking up the stairs. "I hope you like fish, Denzel. We got a bunch of fat ones."

"V," Callie called. "I love this bed. I'm taking it home."

Virginia reached the top of the landing, and turned into the bedroom. "Good luck fitting that on the back of Ernie's snowmobile."

Callie spread out in the bed, stretching. "I should have just stayed up to fight the jet lag, huh?"

Virginia lay down on top of the covers, next to Callie. Denzel hopped on to the blankets covering Callie and licked her face.

Callie pulled her arms up to Denzel to stroke him, and defend herself. "I can see how you fell in love with this place. How was ice fishing?"

Virginia closed her eyes, resting her hands on her breasts. "Unique." She took a deep breath. "It was my first time clubbing something to death."

"Whoa, girl." Callie chuckled. She looked over at Virginia. They shared a moment. "You didn't miss anything back in the tar pits. Same faces, same stories."

Virginia held Callie's gaze.

Denzel seized this opportunity to sandwich himself between the two of them and dig into the blankets with his paws.

"You going to be okay when we get back?" The lines of concern in Callie's face betrayed her Botox with her head sideways on the pillow.

"I had this revelation," Virginia swallowed. "About me. About everyone, I guess."

Callie nodded.

"We're all just characters trying to play our scenes right," Virginia licked her dry lips. "But the thing about life is that you can change the script without anyone throwing a shit fit."

"For sure," Callie agreed.

Virginia inhaled deeply. "And I want you to know how the character you play in my script is exactly what I need: rehab, the cabin, the affirmations. I thought they were stupid, and I only did them because you told me I would think they were stupid. It made me think about how predictable I am."

Denzel snored.

"See?" Virginia pointed at Denzel, and laughed. "All the wild child bullshit pranks were fun, but nothing I was doing was anything new, or cutting edge. I don't even remember half the chicks I hooked up with. It's like some hack was writing my life story, and I was just playing along."

Virginia laid her arm over Denzel. "Anyway, I feel like I'm in charge now. I think it took this long being sober, and saying I love myself, I'm beautiful, and I'm worthy, until I felt like I needed to puke."

Callie's eyes were glossy. "I can't believe I'm hearing this from someone in their twenties. You're fucking wise beyond your years, girl."

They lay there gazing into each other's eyes like only old friends can do.

Virginia lowered her voice. "Would you fuck Sage if you could?"

"Is she here?" Callie half lifted her head. "Did she say something?"

"Nope."

Callie dropped back down to the pillow. "What do you mean by fuck? Like, specifically what does that involve when you have two women? And before you answer that question – probably yes."

Virginia laughed. "I thought you were flirting earlier."

Callie blushed. "I was just being polite."

"Polite might get you laid in the right company," Virginia took a deep breath. "Sage invited us over for a nice dinner tonight. I assumed you would want to go, so I accepted the offer."

Callie worked her way out from under the blanket. "You assumed correctly. Do I have time to shower? And can we stop at the store beforehand? I'm going to hop in the shower."

Callie stripped down, setting her clothes on top of her suitcase. Her bra caught on her rock hard nipples. "Girl you weren't lying about this house being cold. Once you get out from under those blankets, it's colder than a witches teat!"

Virginia rolled off the bed, and went to the closet. She tossed Callie a soft robe, with a wide sash. "So, the word fuck could mean a number of interesting things, it just depends on what girl you ask."

Sage slipped the robe on, and shivered. "Seriously though, did Sage say something?"

Virginia pointed her finger. "Callie's got a crush on my lady!"

Denzel's ears perked up. He rolled over on the bed, and realized he was alone.

"I'll go start on some side dishes for tonight," Virginia walked to the door. "And no, we can't go to the store, but we don't really need anything."

Denzel hopped off the bed, trailing Virginia down the stairs. Cooking came second nature to her at this point, the mind and hands working quickly, and cooperatively to create delicious, healthy foods. Need arose partly from the desperation of living broke and alone when she was a young runaway, partly because healthy food is hard to come by in restaurants if you weren't in the right hipster locales.

By the time the water pipes announced the end of Callie's shower, a trilogy of delights was elegantly plated, and plastic wrapped: green beans fried in olive oil and garlic, topped with cheddar cheese and toasted almonds; a homemade romaine Caesar with apple wedges, and flash toasted croutons; and melted buttery soft carrots in maple glaze with fresh dill.

"I can smell that from up here!" Callie called down from the second story.

In a few minutes, she was down the stairs, wrapped in two towels. "Do you mind if I snack a little before we go?"

Virginia handed Callie her own neatly arranged plate of snacks, already waiting for her.

Callie popped fresh raspberries into her mouth. "You're going to make some woman very happy one day."

"Hopefully tonight." Virginia smirked.

"You sure I won't be a third wheel?" Callie popped a date in her mouth, savoring the soft sweetness.

"Doesn't matter," Virginia held a date in her delicate fingers. "I want you to be there, and also it's a perfect opportunity to schmooze with your crush."

Callie blushed.

Virginia picked up the plastic wrapped plates, and carried them to the door. "Now let's get up there before the sun goes down. Then it gets really cold."

She found an extra thick coat, and a spare pair of snow boots for Callie.

Callie followed her, mouth open. "Colder than this?"

Virginia nodded, and handed her the gear. She slipped the ski mask over her head, then pulled up a hood over that.

They marched in silence once they got outside, both of their faces wrapped in masks. Callie dragged her boots through the snow, letting out the equivalent of a long, low pitched growling sound, or what might have just been a ten-minute ode to 'fuck.'

At Sage's house, Virginia knocked while opening the door, and they popped inside.

"Oh it's like a million degrees warmer in here," Callie chattered. "I think it's actually warmer than your place."

Virginia removed her snow gear, walking toward the kitchen. "Yep."

Sage clanged a spoon against a pan. "Come on in! Dinner's almost ready."

Virginia planted a long slow kiss on Sage's lips. "Mmm, I'm so hungry."

Sage winked at her. "Where's Bartleby?"

Virginia glanced back toward her house. "He was sleeping so soundly, doing that cute little tongue partway out of his cute little mouth. I couldn't bear to wake him up."

Sage mocked a frown.

Callie looked around the cramped studio space, as she made her way around it. "Your house is so... efficient." She set Virginia's side dish plates on the small counter space in the kitchen. "I apologize for not bringing a bottle of wine."

Sage reached for two glasses from a high cabinet. "Not a problem, we have whiskey." She poured two tall drinks, and handed one to Callie.

Callie looked into the translucent amber. "I don't usually drink hard alcohol. I'm kind of a lightweight."

Sage clinked her glass to Callie's. "Welcome to Wisconsin. We do what we can to stay warm." She brought the glass to her playful upturned mouth.

Callie gingerly sipped from her glass, then opened her mouth. "Wah! That's strong! You don't have anything to cut it, do you?"

"Sure," Sage opened the freezer and shook out two ice cubes from a tray. She plunked them into Callie's glass.

Callie took another sip, trying her best not to cringe.

"So," Sage used her oversized metal stirring spoon as a pointer. "We have baked trout in a maple lemon reduction, pan seared walleye with winter chives, and bluegill hush puppies, with my famous homemade ranch to dip them in."

She leaned over and opened the oven, dodging her head to the side as steam billowed out. "And good old fashioned cornbread."

Callie finished her whiskey. "You're speaking my language, girl. Let's do this before I burst from excitement!"

Sage filled up Callie's whiskey glass again, making it a double this time.

They plated their meals, and then took them to the chairs in the living room.

Everyone quietly feasted on the abundance of delicacies.

Virginia held up a piece of cornbread, torn in half, a pat of butter drizzling down the face of it. "This is the best cornbread I've ever had."

"Mmm," Callie nodded in agreement. She chewed, and swallowed her fish. "I agree, and I'm from the South. What's your recipe?"

A self-satisfied grin beamed on Sage' face. "I chop up fresh corn and stir it with grass-fed butter. I know an Amish family up here, and I get the best butter you've ever had."

Virginia stuck her index finger in the air, finishing another bite of cornbread. "Yes, the absolute best butter."

Sage poured another whiskey for Callie as she ran low.

They finished up casually, their bellies full.

"I don't get much company around here," Sage mused. "I appreciate it."

"That meal was worth the flight up." Callie slurred her mild Southern twang. "But you two don't need me around for a game of spades, or whatever you had planned for later."

"You want me to walk you back?" Virginia pointed to the window. Dusk had grown into a fully dark night, the snow gently swirling in the light cast through the glass.

"Oh, please." Callie flapped her hand too hard in the air. "I can handle myself."

Virginia stood up, and offered Callie a hand. "That's what I thought until I almost died out there. I might not be here right now if I didn't have Sage to rescue me."

Sage smiled. "Speaking of which, maybe I should be the one to walk her home."

Virginia shrugged. "I won't fight you on that."

Sage helped Callie bundle up her floppy arms, and the two of them were out the door.

Virginia assessed the mess situation. She stacked the silverware onto the dirty plates, and carried them to the kitchen. She came back for the glasses. She set Sage's full whiskey glass on her desk, then took the other glasses back to the kitchen to wash up the dishes.

The warm water flowed over her hands, soothing alongside the rhythmic circles of the soapy sponge. It was like affirmations: repetitive, meditative, good for the soul. By the time she was done wiping down the stove, the front door handle clicked again.

Sage opened the front door, stomping snow off her boots as she walked in. When she caught Virginia's eye, she shook her head.

Virginia laughed. "Did she try to kiss you, or something?"

Sage pulled her boots off. "Try?" She shook her head again. "Are you sure that lady has a husband?" She delicately unstrapped her backpack, and Denzel pounced out as it neared the ground.

Virginia laughed again, drying her hands. She glided across the room with the hand towel. "Every woman is flexible under the right circumstances. And Callie's ladyboner for you is pretty obvious."

21

Last Night

Virginia helped unzip Sage's jacket, sliding it down her shoulders. "Feels like it's cold out there. We need to warm you up." She slipped both hands into Sage's snow pants, pushing them down to her ankles as she traced kisses over the fabric of Sage's shirt.

Denzel rammed his head into the side of Virginia's leg. He licked her toes, then circled up, and ran for the comfort of the living room chair.

"Sorry about my friend," Virginia nibbled on the meat of Sage's inner thighs. "Is there any way I can make it up to you?" She peered up from where she rested on her knees, the bottom half of her face hidden under Sage's black thong.

Sage reached down to tuck Virginia's hair behind her ear. "There is nothing you need to be sorry for."

Virginia hooked her fingers into Sage's panty line, pulling the bottom to the side. Her warm mouth enveloped Sage, gently tonguing her ridges.

Sage leaned back against the door, her hands already on Virginia's head pulling her in closer.

Virginia coated Sage evenly with her thick spit, mingling their juices. Her eager tongue darted into Sage's increasingly juicy peach, thrumming with pleasure. She tilted her head back, matching the curve of her chin to Sage's pelvis.

Sage flailed for something to hold onto, and stuck her hand into the door handle. She tried to lift her legs up through the snow pants wrapped around her ankles, but Virginia firmly planted her knee in the middle, pinning them to the ground.

Virginia twisted her fingers holding the bottom of the thong, and they tightened like a tourniquet.

"Oh!" Sage's butt cheeks clenched, her hand instinctually grabbing for Virginia's hair.

Virginia emanated a deep, throaty laugh, her mouth still sealed around Sage.

Sage's knees shook. "Oh, wow."

Virginia looped her fingers again, and Sage's thong threatened to burst at the seams. The fleshy part of Sage's tender area bulged over one side of the fabric, and Virginia caressed it gently with her mouth.

She pushed Sage back into the door until there was no space left.

Sage grabbed the door handle harder, her other hand on Virginia's head, guiding it home. She tried to open her legs wider, but her ankles were still firmly trapped in her snow pants. The pressure of her shaky legs squeezing together was bringing up something visceral, deep, and beyond any pleasure she'd felt before.

Virginia relentlessly dove into it with her errant tongue, keeping firm pressure, and a steady rhythm. Her fingers cramped with the thong twisted around them, her fingertip turning purple from a lack of oxygen.

Sage's body convulsed, twisting as her knees gave out and her weight dropped her into Virginia's mouth. She moaned long, and loud.

Virginia backed up enough for Sage to slide down the door until her butt reached the ground. She didn't break contact until Sage's muscle spasms stopped.

Sage looked up at the ceiling, her mouth open. An aftershock rippled through her thighs. "That was unbelievable. I think I'm still cumming." Another jolt tingled down her spine, all the way to her feet. She swept her feet out from underneath her, as Virginia backed away.

Virginia slid Sage's pants, and panties over her ankles, and tossed them aside. "Do you mind if I stay the night?"

Sage lifted her head to see Virginia. "I would mind if you didn't stay the night."

Virginia crawled forward, and planted her juicy mouth on Sage's.

Sage could taste her natural flavorings on Virginia's lips. "Mmm. Can we go back to the fact that your friend kissed me?"

Virginia shrugged sheepishly.

Sage smiled, her head askance. "Is that her party trick, or something?"

Virginia ran her fingertips down Sage's legs. "I would just chalk it up to the fact that you, my dear, are irresistible."

"Hardly," Sage chuckled. "Maybe it was the whiskey." She shivered again as Virginia's ticklish fingertip strokes lightly painted her lower half.

Virginia pushed one hand into the ground, and found her feet. She lowered her other hand, offering it to Sage. "Are you comfy on the floor, or do you want to go up to the loft?"

Sage reluctantly accepted Virginia's hand, and stood up. "Sounds like a plan. I need some water first." She made her way to the kitchen and filled up two metal water bottles.

Virginia followed Sage up the stairs to the loft. She wondered if she would ever be here again. Tonight might be a goodbye to Sage, to this house, and to the eerie, snowy, winter of Lost Hollow Lake. She came here a judgmental mess, and was leaving on good terms with the people, and the place.

Success.

Denzel lifted his head as their bare feet resounded on the metal spiral stairs. He hopped off the chair, and followed them up to the loft, his nails plinking on the metal as he hopped.

Sage rolled into bed. "I want to do something amazing to you too, but I'm so sleepy. Can I dream something up and have my way with you in the morning?"

Virginia crawled into bed sideways, resting her head on Sage's thigh. "That sounds delightful. But I'm going to want a piece of you, too."

Denzel reached the top of the landing, and pounced onto the bed. He licked Virginia's ribs.

Virginia laughed aloud, and curled her arm around Denzel, bringing him in close.

Sage closed her eyes. "Deal."

"I know you're tired, so it's not a good time to talk," Virginia paused.

Sage stared up at the slope in the roof above them.

Denzel rolled over, and pushed his paws into Virginia's side. He flipped his head upside down, and relaxed into the blankets. His cute little tongue hung out a tiny bit, defying gravity.

Virginia turned her face toward Sage's head. "Callie found me a perfect role, and I'm really excited about it."

Sage reached her hand down to Virginia's shoulder and squeezed it. "That's great. I'm excited for you."

"The other part of that is that I'm probably leaving tomorrow to go home."

The two women sat on that information, weighing out the implications.

Virginia broke the silence. "I've really enjoyed the time I spent with you."

"Yeah," Sage said softly. "I thought we might have a little more."

"I know it hasn't been that long, and I don't want to seem crazy for suggesting it," Virginia sucked in, ready to spill. "Is it weird to get all serious right now?"

Sage yawned. "No less weird than every other interaction we've had up until this point."

At that, Denzel kicked his legs spastically, sleeping, and probably dreaming already.

"I just try to live life as chill as possible." Virginia took a deep breath, exhaling slowly. "I don't want to seem overly dramatic."

Sage patted Virginia's head. "You literally enact drama for a living."

Virginia let that sink in.

"I don't suppose I could come back here for a play date with Denzel?"

Sage laughed. "Only if you call him Bartleby."

Virginia kept at it, tentatively. "I was thinking that maybe you and Bartleby would like to come visit LA, get some sun. You can borrow my SPF-fifty. We even have snow. You have to go up to the mountains, like Big Bear, or Mammoth, but you could get your fix."

"I have to be honest with you, too," Sage's voice was cool.

Virginia flinched, one eye squinting.

"I don't even like snow," Sage cupped her hand behind Virginia's shoulder. "Talk about weird, right? Lost Hollow Lake reminds me of the last time I felt like a whole person, back when my dad was around. I don't know why I stuck around this long – nostalgia maybe. It's been like living through one long punishment I thought I deserved for something that ultimately wasn't even my fault."

Virginia lit up. "So you're coming?"

"I'm not big into commitment," Sage chose her words carefully. "But I'm not staying here forever. A little sunshine might do us good."

22

Back in Action

The sky was cloudless, save the thick layer of smog that permanently loomed over the City of Angels built over tar pits filled with the distant remains of predatory dinosaurs. The sun shone with the force to break a dry sweat, and push skin cells into replicating too quickly.

Virginia leaned against the thick canvas edge of her chair, watching people mill around the set with an endless string of small, unimportant tasks. A woman her size and weight, but with a homely face sat in a similar chair, ten paces away. She was chain smoking, and talking to herself as though she had any lines to memorize.

It wasn't unusual for a stand-in to think they were better than the extras because they did get paid more, but this girl wouldn't say a thing to Virginia unless it was work related. Maybe she thought this was her big break, and she would be the up-and-coming starlet in the next few years. It was a dream most girls shared when they first moved here.

Virginia's phone vibrated on the fold-up makeup table nest to her. (715) was the North Woods. She picked it up, and set it on speaker.

"Hi there, Beauty!" Ernie's distinctive voice cut through the static.

"Ernie! What's the news?" Virginia nodded at a young production assistant wearing a hoodie despite the heat, who set a water bottle on the table next to her. The girl gave an awkward bow of the head, and speed walked away.

"News? Nothing new up here. I picked up that extra long grocery list you asked for. Where did you want me to take it?"

Virginia set her phone down, and uncapped the water. "Take it to your house, please. It's all for you." She sipped the cool water. "You there?"

Static. "That's so kind of you. It's too much."

Virginia traded the water bottle for her phone. "It's the least I could do. You're a good man Ernie. You deserve it."

"Thank you." It sounded like he was getting choked up. "You let me know when you come back up here, okay?"

"You'll be the first to know," Virginia said. "Or at least in the top three."

A woman with a makeup palette, and foam dabbers closed in on Virginia. She waited patiently for access to Virginia's face.

"Thank you really, truly," Ernie said. "You radio me any time, okay?"

"Okay, bye my dear." Virginia nodded, and the makeup lady moved in with gentle strokes, eradicating shine.

"Any word on when they actually need me?" Virginia talked through clenched teeth, keeping any facial skin movement to a minimum.

The makeup lady switched to a powder brush, swooshing broad circles around Virginia's cheeks. "Nope." Her single word was drawn out to the speed of an entire sentence, like she needed to keep her own face still for the magic of makeup to work on Virginia.

She let her brush hand drop, inspecting Virginia's face from way too close into her personal bubble. Satisfied, she turned, and walked away.

Virginia shook out her manicured mane, flipping it to one side, then the other. She stood up, and stretched. Callie warned her to look for a surprise on set today, to which the most obvious conclusion would be Sage. But Callie was full of surprises.

Still, Virginia was on edge since the 6:00 a.m. call. She scanned the crowd yet again, her breathing shallow. Through the mass of people, one woman's face stood out.

Sage turned. She was rocking a smart ribbed top cut like a vest, the form hugging her voluptuous features. Her platinum hair fit in with a majority of the women on set, though she was the only natural. Her pale skin set her apart from the hybrid artificial tans surrounding her. Her lack of surgeries lent an air of authentic realism to her beauty.

It was the first time Virginia had seen Sage in anything other than snow gear, lounge sweats, or her birthday suit. Her classic beauty was only shadowed by her commanding presence. All conversation stopped when she turned to fix her gaze on Virginia.

Virginia's heart fluttered. Her low-cut tunic didn't leave much to the imagination, other than what everyone imagined they would do with her if they were able to get that tunic off. Her skinny jeans showed off the defined curvature of her sleek legs. Even her unadorned feet, bare between takes, begged for a second glance.

"You made it down okay?" Virginia's question came out more like a statement. She walked tentatively closer to Sage.

Sage stepped closer still. "I got in late last night." A moment passed. "I didn't want to be presumptuous."

Virginia closed the distance between them. She extended her hand. "Please, be as presumptuous as you'd like."

Sage stepped in, brushing Virginia's hand to the side. She offered her lips.

Virginia took the bait, cutting through the awkwardness of a first kiss in a new location. The heat melted any inhibitions in a heartbeat, and she leaned in for the real deal.

Sage held her ground, leaning down as she swept an arm behind Virginia, pulling her in closer. Her other hand instinctively clapped down on Virginia's skinny jeans. The second kiss lasted much longer, leaving a sexy string of spit between their lips.

Virginia pulled Sage toward her as a tall man holding two long metal poles with wide, solid bases pushed his way past them. "Thanks for coming to the set. It's always a little crazy around here."

Sage shrugged casually. "Callie told me to meet her here with Dana."

"Dana Bruzontti?" Virginia's eyes widened. "She was serious about selling anything you wrote in a heartbeat, huh?"

"I take it Dana is some big shot around here?"

"Dana produced a little film called 'Down Five Grey,' which did over half a billion dollars at the box office. Oh, and it was based off a book." She jabbed her finger playfully into Sage's cleavage. "You seriously need to watch more movies, especially now that you're here."

Sage clapped her hand over Virginia's, trapping it against her chest. "It might be nice to sit down to relax after that long ride. And I do like popcorn."

Virginia pressed her chest against Sage's, reclaiming her hand. "If that's an invitation to cuddle, then you're coming over to my place after we wrap. I even have bison steaks in the freezer for you and Bartleby."

"About that," Sage smoothed the back of her hair. "I Googled Denzel."

"Oh yeah?"

Sage nodded. "Yeah. It's cute. I like it."

Virginia raised up her shoulders and closed her eyes, squeezing Sage's hand.

"Every time we went for a walk, he ran down to your cabin to come see you." Sage held Virginia's gaze. "And we were both sad you weren't home." Her eyes trailed off to the side. "Is Dana a man, by any chance?"

Virginia laughed out loud as she looked over her shoulder.

Callie was walking toward them with Dana Bruzontti, a slick-haired middle-aged man with broad shoulders, a trimmed thick beard, and a kind smile. Everything about him seemed casually expensive without trying to make a statement. Callie was dressed to the nines, her rock star top keeping her augmented breasts in place.

Callie kissed Virginia on the cheek, then blushed as she kissed Sage on the cheek as well. "Nice to see you again, Sage. This is Dana."

Dana offered a slow, warm handshake to Sage, then Virginia. He made sincere eye contact, and didn't jump right into speaking – an anomaly for his locale, and profession. "I can't thank Callie enough for setting up this meeting. You've both been on my radar for some time, and I would love to have you all for a chill private dinner." He used his hands smartly, with broad, confident gestures.

Virginia smiled. "Speaking for myself, I'm glad we didn't meet until now. I am over my rough patch." She looked over at Sage. "Dinner sounds great to me."

Sage nodded in agreement. "It's good to put a face with a name. I'd much rather meet somewhere cooler, so dinner sounds good to me, as well."

Dana clapped. "Alright! That was way too easy." He fixed his eyes on Sage. "I know you're new here, and it can be intimidating at first. You're in good hands already, but you can call me any time if you need anything. Okay?"

"That's very kind of you," Sage clapped Dana on the shoulder.

Dana nodded to the Director's tent, where a crowd of people huddled around a bank of monitors. "I'm going to go pop in and pay my respects. Again, it was a pleasure. I look forward to some real conversation soon, I want to hear more about all of you." He waved as he took a step backward, and turned.

Sage looked between Callie and Virginia. "Was that our whole meeting? Did I miss something?"

Callie pulled out her phone. "That was it! His studio already sent the numbers, and I think you're going to like them a lot. I retained as much creative control on your end as possible." She tapped her phone, then held the screen up for Sage to see. "Here, I just sent it to you."

Sage bit her lip as she looked at the screen. "That's for one book?"

"Yep." A satisfied smile crept across Callie's face. "And you probably don't know how impressive it is that I got you residuals, and a cut of the gross." She pointed to her phone. "This is just the start."

"Kind of overwhelming," Sage shifted her weight uncomfortably. "I'm going back to my hotel room, with Denzel. All these people are giving me some mild social anxiety."

Virginia put on a faux pouty face.

Sage slipped her a card key with the hotel emblem on it. "Come by afterwards, or we'll come to your place."

Virginia snuck in a long, slow kiss. "Deal. See you soon."

Sage tossed a wave to Callie, then walked away.

"I owe you," Callie mock-punched Virginia in the shoulder.

Virginia laughed. "You're kidding, right? I wouldn't be on this set, or with that woman if it weren't for you." She exhaled deeply. "I might not even be alive."

"Okay, then we'll call it even." Callie brought Virginia in for a tight hug. "You know what?" She lowered her voice, her mouth next to Virginia's ear. "I know everything is all fairy tale perfect right now, but monsters have a way of popping back up when you least expect them."

Virginia nodded, her face buried in Callie's shoulder.

Callie drew her head back to make eye contact with Virginia. "Girl, you let me know if you feel that darkness coming back, you hear?"

Virginia sniffled, her eyes glossy. "Yep."

The End

A Note From the Author

Thank you for reading *Rescue*, I truly appreciate it. If you liked the story, please take thirty seconds to leave a review on Amazon! I read and treasure every book review. If you have ten seconds to share the book on social media, I would truly appreciate that too. Word of mouth is still the way we all find things we like these days, and you might really be helping someone out.

I'm always trying to grow as a person, and as an author. If you want to contact me directly, send an email to julietterenardauthor@gmail.com and I will get back to you when possible.

Books by Juliette Renard:

Blood of the Sun: When an Amazon adventure guide dies from a centipede bite, a group of foreigners need to find their way back to civilization. As they forge through the jungle, they discover a dark secret about the Brazilian government, while the women grow a lot closer than any of them expected.

Rescue: When a puppy mysteriously shows up on Virginia's rehab cabin doorstep in the middle of a snowstorm, it helps her to reevaluate what she holds important in life. When the puppy's owner finds her, she's brought into an unfamiliar and dangerous game that might sidetrack her from staying out of trouble.

Here's a sample chapter from **Blood of the Sun**:

Amazon River Basin, Brazil

Beads of sweat glinted in the firelight, dripping over a little shadow crawling up the wrinkled skin of the dark man's cheek. Omagalu's glossy eyes strained to follow the path of the black centipede stretched across his face, its body melding with his own skin the color of night. The back of the man's head pressed into the jungle mud, strained so long now that the nerves at the nape of his neck pinched.

The centipede moved forward a finger's width, its dozens of legs creeping over his skin. Its mandibles opened and closed, searching for the softest spot to puncture.

Six figures loomed over him in the darkness.

A young woman with dirty, red curly locks matted to her sunburned Northern complexion knelt by his side, leaning closer. "He's trying to say don't do it," Rebecca said in a calm, muted voice. The firelight flickered her soft features alive.

Omagalu whimpered, the words inaudible. His body and head remained motionless, save the tired shaking from holding still for too long.

"No way," said the man kneeling next to her. Brad poised a stick at the centipede. "He's telling me to hurry up and do it already." He inched his muscular torso forward, closing the gap between he and the sleek monster, while shouldering Rebecca out of the equation.

Behind them, another young woman leaned in, her short blond hair hiding her eyes. "Do you think it's poisonous?" Lina whispered.

"Everything in the Amazon is poisonous," replied Rebecca. "Did you read any guidebooks before you landed here?"

Yuri, a middle aged, tall, rotund man, shushed gently through his big, pursed lips. "He tell us all to be quiet. Animal sense fear." His Russian accent was thick, but comprehensible.

"I'm sensing fear from all of you animals," joked Brad. "At least one of us here has the balls to man up and do this." He slowed his progress to a near halt, the stick now so close to the back of the centipede it was almost touching the chitin armor. The centipede paused, halfway over Omagalu's nose, as though it could sense danger.

Omagalu's unblinking eyes darted from the centipede to the stick, tears squeezing out the corners. His breathy guttural noises came faster and louder.

"Seriously, if you piss off that centipede," whispered Rebecca, "he could get stung and maybe even die. And for the record, a centipede isn't an animal. It's an arthropod."

"And if you don't shut up, this insect is going to bite him, and kill him anyway," Brad replied.

He thrust the stick forward and whacked the centipede on the side, sending it flying into the sticks and underbrush surrounding them.

Brad smiled and stood up. "See? Problem solved! You're welcome."

Below them, Omagalu opened his mouth and let out a low moan. His eyes closed and he shivered spastically.

Rebecca opened her canteen, and leaned in toward Omagalu. "Are you okay? Did it get you?" She bent down and attended to him.

Lina shuddered and used her shaky finger to swipe her phone screen, shining her flashlight over the scene.

Their gear lay neatly packed in a row of six backpacks. Surrounding them, six lean-to tents conjoined at the center, where a fire burned low.

Standing a respectful distance from the crowd, a woman watched in silence. Her strong, dark silhouette stayed stoic throughout the incident. Even now, Ti folded her arms around herself, observing.

An enormous, rotund man rested his tired thumbs in his bountiful waistline. He watched the movement in the night like a disinterested taskmaster.

Rebecca poured water gently over Omagalu's lips, but he wouldn't open his mouth.

An older man hovered over Rebecca. He fumbled through the dark, squatting down until he was face to face with her. Ernie held out a sandwich.

"He doesn't seem to be responding right now, so I don't know if he wants any food." Rebecca pushed in and studied Omagalu's face. "Bring that light closer," she demanded.

Lina stepped closer, losing her footing in the undergrowth. Her phone light swayed wildly around the jungle, then focused on the dark man.

Rebecca prodded at the dark man with her index finger. "What was your name, Omagalu? No bites on your face. Are you okay?" She turned back to the crowd. "Could someone please be on lookout duty?"

"For what?" asked Brad. "The centipede? All I see is that we're surrounded by little six inch black sticks and every one of them looks like they're moving now." He kicked his feet into the sticks, scattering them everywhere, then stomped all around.

Rebecca tilted Omagalu's head back. "Light," she said.

Lina moved around to the other side of her and brought her phone light in closer. She had to lean in and rest her weight on Rebecca to get closer.

"This is bad news," Rebecca said. Her fingers dabbed at two swollen punctures rising from the side of Omagalu's throat.

"I didn't do that," said Brad, moving in to see what she was looking at. "I just flicked the centipede off him."

"Nobody's blaming you," said Rebecca. "But it's still bad news for all of us. Unless any of you are familiar with the Amazon."

Omagalu swallowed and his Adam's apple bobbed, extending the protrusions on his neck to a grotesquely bulbous proportion.

"This is so fucked," said Lina.

"And exciting," added Brad.

Old man Ernie blundered close. "We should make a list and see if he had any enemies that he knew about." Everyone turned to him for a moment, gazing blankly through the darkness. "That's what they do on television, and they usually solve it."

"Just get some more water, please," Rebecca said. "Maybe we can cool him down. He's burning up."

Ernie handed her a canteen.

"Alright, I'm going to administer anti-venom," said Rebecca. "We take shifts and watch our tour guide through the night. In the morning, we cut this adventure short and go back to Manaus. We're only two days away, one if we don't stop to sightsee all the deadly things around us."

Rebecca picked up Omagalu's head, and poured water into her hand, wiping his brow. She rummaged through her backpack and picked out a bottle of medicine. She put two tablets into his mouth, then poured water in. She stroked his throat, mindful of the tender area. The water and pills sloshed out the side of his lips and dribbled down his naked torso.

Rebecca pressed her first two fingers into Omagalu's neck. "Oh shit," she announced.

"What?" Lina tried to shine the light on Rebecca's hand.

"I think this guy is dead," a chill ran down Rebecca's spine. She retracted her hand and shook it off.

They all leaned in for a closer look.

Lina's hand shook as she tried to hold her light steady.

Omagalu's head rolled back, his open eyes reflecting the firelight.

"How are we supposed to get home?" Lina flicked the light off. The question sat heavy in the darkness of night.

Blood of the Sun is available now in print and eBook format on Amazon.com.

40176996R00123

Made in the USA
Middletown, DE
23 March 2019